IN
THE GALAPAGOS ISLANDS
WITH
HERMAN MELVILLE

THE ENCANTADAS
OR
ENCHANTED ISLES

Also by Lynn Michelsohn . . .

*Roswell, Your Travel Guide to the UFO Capital
of the World!*

*Tales from Brookgreen
Folklore, Ghost Stories, and Gullah Folktales
in the South Carolina Lowcountry*

IN

THE GALAPAGOS ISLANDS

WITH

HERMAN MELVILLE

THE ENCANTADAS OR ENCHANTED ISLES

Herman Melville
Lynn Michelsohn
Photographs by Moses Michelsohn

Cleanan Press, Inc.
Roswell, New Mexico

In the Galapagos Islands with Herman Melville
The Encantadas or Enchanted Isles

by Herman Melville, Lynn Michelsohn

New material Copyright © 2011 by Lynn Michelsohn

ISBN: 978-0-9771614-0-9
LCCN: 2011921865

First Edition 1.0

Note: Some longer sections of Melville's writings have been broken into multiple paragraphs to improve readability. His original spelling, grammar, and punctuation have been retained.

Published by: Cleanan Press, Inc.
            106 North Washington Avenue
            Roswell, NM 88201

Visit our website for more information about the Galapagos Islands and our other publications.

www.cleananpress.com

Preface

Visitors have been arriving in the Galapagos Islands since at least 1535. While naturalist Charles Darwin made these volcanic peaks famous, Spanish explorers, English buccaneers (a fancy name for pirates), American whalers, Ecuadorian colonists, and a United States President have all put in appearances here over the centuries.

Herman Melville, author of *Moby-Dick*, was one such visitor. Like many before him, he returned home to write about the strange worlds he found in these Enchanted Isles.

We hope your own stay in the Galapagos Islands is enriched by these glimpses of its captivating natural and human history written over 150 years ago by that famous fellow visitor.

Lynn Michelsohn
Moses Michelsohn

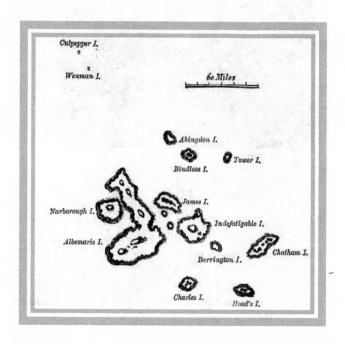

The Galapagos
Islands

Table of Contents

Introduction

Moby-Dick *was a failure.*

"So much trash" and a "monstrous bore" proclaimed the nicest critics.

Sales were poor.

Even greater scorn greeted his next novel, Pierre. *"HERMAN MELVILLE CRAZY" blasted one New York review . . . and he had tried so hard to make this a romantic—even sentimental—story that would appeal to the book-buying public. Instead, it grew to encompass challenging themes and innovative forms. Now, it too was failing . . .*

* * *

Herman Melville's career had started with such promise. His first two novels, Typee *(1846) and* Omoo *(1847), quickly became bestsellers. These titillating debut novels, filled with embellished accounts of his own youthful adventures after deserting the New Bedford whaler* Acushnet *in the South Seas, caught the public's fancy both in England and America. Critical and financial success foretold a brilliant future.*

Melville soon wooed and married Lizzie Shaw, the only daughter of Massachusetts' Supreme Court Chief Justice. He purchased a small farm in the idyllic Berkshire Mountains. His emotional and financial struggles that had followed the bankruptcy and early death of his father, a once-wealthy New York businessman, seemed over.

But Melville wanted to make a positive impact on the world with his writing. He began to focus on serious issues: political injustice, human cruelty, religious intolerance, slavery, racial bigotry, and the rigid sexual mores of his time.

He set his third novel, Mardi *(1849), in the South Seas once again but this time explored intensely political and highly philosophical issues. Melville considered it his masterpiece. Critics called it "a rubbishing rhapsody," "a tissue of conceits," and "a mass of downright nonsense." Not surprisingly, sales were disappointing.*

Perhaps simpler and more readable stories would regain him readers? He wrote Redburn *(1849) about his first voyage as a cabin boy and* White Jacket *(1850) drawing on his year as a Navy seaman. But satirical criticism of the institutions he despised crept into these works as well; fans did not return.*

The reading public loved exotic tales set in exotic places. Strong heroic characters, direct action, romanticized locales, and suggestive "physicality" were popular literary motifs. Allegorical attacks on religious or political evils and innovative explorations of ambiguous aspects of the human condition most certainly were not.

Still determined to address important themes, Melville went on to write Moby-Dick *(1851) and* Pierre *(1852), losing readers with each new novel. Royalties decreased pitifully. By the end of 1853 he had yet to recoup publication costs for* Pierre—*his publishers had stopped absorbing these charges as his popularity declined . . .*

Now, as 1854 began, the thirty-four year old author was supporting his growing family on borrowed money and advances from his wife's expected inheritance. His moodiness increased with his alcohol intake as attacks of sciatica threatened chronic pain. Although he delighted in the antics of his two young sons, relations with his wife grew ever more strained.

Family members pressured him to give up writing. "Use the good education you received as a youth," his demanding mother probably urged. "Take a diplomatic post like your brother!" (her beloved, successful older son whose early death had once again robbed her of her life of ease).

Throughout that icy Massachusetts winter, Melville struggled to regain his readership with shorter and less challenging magazine articles. Hour after hour he scratched away at his cramped writing desk until each early dusk interrupted his efforts.

By January of 1854, Melville had begun to construct a series of ten sketches—really an extended travelogue—full of myth and exotic scenery but still reflecting complex themes of good and evil that dominated his thoughts. And Putnam's Monthly Magazine had agreed to buy the stories at $5 a page! He could feel his career coming back to life.

Once more he transported himself away from the snowy blasts that rattled his Pittsfield farmhouse; back twelve years and three thousand miles to the tropical South Seas of his youth.

Could he bring readers along with him to that archipelago with the wonderfully alluring name, "The Enchanted Isles"? Could he blend his own experiences with stories from the forecastle and tales told by other adventurers to recreate that alien realm where the Acushnet had once put in for fresh water and tortoise steaks? Could he recapture his lost popularity with these sketches of the Galapagos Islands?

Decide for yourself . . .

One

Herman Melville clearly has no place writing travel brochures. His bleak depiction of volcanic Galapagos landscapes would certainly not entice tourists seeking a tropical paradise.

And he quickly dispels any Disney-like associations with the archipelago's nickname by conveying the understanding that Encantada was used in its negative sense of "bewitched" rather than intending any more joyful connotation.

Yet this first of four sketches describing the natural world of the Galapagos Islands (and beginning, like most of the ten, with a quote from Edmund Spenser's The Faerie Queen), with its images of stark volcanic islands populated by demonic creatures—all probably a reflection of his own dark psyche—prepares visitors still today in an (almost) realistic way for their upcoming experiences.

What better introduction could there be to the other-worldly environment of the Enchanted Isles?

SKETCH FIRST.
THE ISLES AT LARGE.

—"That may not be, said then the ferryman,
Least we unweeting hap to be fordonne;
For those same islands seeming now and than,
Are not firme land, nor any certein wonne,
But stragling plots which to and fro do ronne
In the wide waters; therefore are they hight
The Wandering Islands; therefore do them shonne;
For they have oft drawne many a wandring wight
Into most deadly daunger and distressed plight;
For whosoever once hath fastened
His foot thereon may never it secure
But wandreth evermore uncertein and unsure."

"Darke, dolefull, dreary, like a greedy grave,
That still for carrion carcasses doth crave;
On top whereof ay dwelt the ghastly owl,
Shrieking his balefull note, which ever drave
Far from that haunt all other cheerful fowl,
And all about it wandring ghosts did wayle and howl."

Take five-and-twenty heaps of cinders dumped here and there in an outside city lot; imagine some of them magnified into mountains, and the vacant lot the sea; and you will have a fit idea of the general aspect of the Encantadas, or Enchanted Isles. A group rather of extinct volcanoes than of isles; looking much as the world at large might, after a penal conflagration.

It is to be doubted whether any spot of earth can, in desolateness, furnish a parallel to this group. Abandoned cemeteries of long ago, old cities by piecemeal tumbling to their ruin, these are melancholy enough; but, like all else which has but once been associated with humanity, they still awaken in us some thoughts of sympathy, however sad. Hence, even the Dead Sea, along with whatever other emotions it may at times inspire, does not fail to touch in the pilgrim some of his less unpleasurable feelings.

And as for solitariness; the great forests of the north, the expanses of unnavigated waters, the Greenland ice-fields, are the profoundest of solitudes to a human observer; still the magic of their changeable tides and seasons mitigates their terror; because, though unvisited by men, those forests are visited by the May; the remotest seas reflect familiar stars even as Lake Erie does; and in the clear air of a fine Polar day, the irradiated, azure ice shows beautifully as malachite.

But the special curse, as one may call it, of the Encantadas, that which exalts them in desolation above Idumea and the Pole, is, that to them change never comes; neither the change of seasons nor of sorrows. Cut by the Equator, they know not autumn, and they know not spring; while already reduced to the lees of fire, ruin itself can work little more upon them.

The showers refresh the deserts; but in these isles, rain never falls. Like split Syrian gourds left withering in the sun, they are cracked by an everlasting drought beneath a torrid sky. "Have mercy upon me," the wailing spirit of the Encantadas seems to cry, "and send Lazarus that he may dip the tip of his finger in water and cool my tongue, for I am tormented in this flame."

Another feature in these isles is their emphatic uninhabitableness. It is deemed a fit type of all-forsaken overthrow, that the jackal should den in the wastes of weedy Babylon; but the Encantadas refuse to harbor even the outcasts of the beasts. Man and wolf alike disown them. Little but reptile life is here found: tortoises, lizards, immense spiders, snakes, and that strangest anomaly of outlandish nature, the *aguano*. No voice, no low, no howl is heard; the chief sound of life here is a hiss.

On most of the isles where vegetation is found at all, it is more ungrateful than the blankness of Aracama. Tangled thickets of wiry bushes, without fruit and without a name, springing up among deep fissures of calcined rock, and treacherously masking them; or a parched growth of distorted cactus trees.

In many places the coast is rock-bound, or, more properly, clinker-bound; tumbled masses of blackish or greenish stuff like the dross of an iron-furnace, forming dark clefts and caves here and there, into which a ceaseless sea pours a fury of foam; overhanging them with a swirl of gray, haggard mist, amidst which sail screaming flights of unearthly birds heightening the dismal din. However calm the sea without, there is no rest for these swells and those rocks; they lash and are lashed, even when the outer ocean is most at peace with, itself.

On the oppressive, clouded days, such as are peculiar to this part of the watery Equator, the dark, vitrified masses, many of which raise themselves among white whirlpools and breakers in detached and perilous places off the shore, present a most Plutonian sight. In no world but a fallen one could such lands exist.

Those parts of the strand free from the marks of fire, stretch away in wide level beaches of multitudinous dead shells, with here and there decayed bits of sugar-cane, bamboos, and cocoanuts, washed upon this other and darker world from the charming palm isles to the westward and southward; all the way from Paradise to Tartarus; while mixed with the relics of distant beauty you will sometimes see fragments of charred wood and mouldering ribs of wrecks.

Neither will any one be surprised at meeting these last, after observing the conflicting currents which eddy throughout nearly all the wide channels of the entire group. The capriciousness of the tides of air sympathizes with those of the sea. Nowhere is the wind so light, baffling, and every way unreliable, and so given to perplexing calms, as at the Encantadas.

Nigh a month has been spent by a ship going from one isle to another, though but ninety miles between; for owing to the force of the current, the boats employed to tow barely suffice to keep the craft from sweeping upon the cliffs, but do nothing towards accelerating her voyage.

Sometimes it is impossible for a vessel from afar to fetch up with the group itself, unless large allowances for prospective lee-way have been made ere its coming in sight. And yet, at other times, there is a mysterious indraft, which irresistibly draws a passing vessel among the isles, though not bound to them.

True, at one period, as to some extent at the present day, large fleets of whalemen cruised for spermaceti upon what some seamen call the Enchanted Ground. But this, as in due place will be described, was off the great outer isle of Albemarle [Isabela], away from the intricacies of the smaller isles, where there is plenty of sea-room; and hence, to that vicinity, the above remarks do not altogether apply; though even there the current runs at times with singular force, shifting, too, with as singular a caprice.

Indeed, there are seasons when currents quite unaccountable prevail for a great distance round about the total group, and are so strong and irregular as to change a vessel's course against the helm, though sailing at the rate of four or five miles the hour.

The difference in the reckonings of navigators, produced by these causes, along with the light and variable winds, long nourished a persuasion, that there existed two distinct clusters of isles in the parallel of the Encantadas, about a hundred leagues apart. Such was the idea of their earlier visitors, the Buccaneers; and as late as 1750, the charts of that part of the Pacific accorded with the strange delusion. And this apparent fleetingness and unreality of the locality of the isles was most probably one reason for the Spaniards calling them the Encantada, or Enchanted Group.

But not uninfluenced by their character, as they now confessedly exist, the modern voyager will be inclined to fancy that the bestowal of this name might have in part originated in that air of spell-bound desertness which so significantly invests the isles. Nothing can better suggest the aspect of once living things malignly crumbled from ruddiness into ashes. Apples of Sodom, after touching, seem these isles.

However wavering their place may seem by reason of the currents, they themselves, at least to one upon the shore, appear invariably the same: fixed, cast, glued into the very body of cadaverous death.

Nor would the appellation, enchanted, seem misapplied in still another sense. For concerning the peculiar reptile inhabitant of these wilds—whose presence gives the group its second Spanish name, Gallipagos—concerning the tortoises found here, most mariners have long cherished a superstition, not more frightful than grotesque. They earnestly believe that all wicked sea-officers, more especially commodores and captains, are at death (and, in some cases, before death) transformed into tortoises; thenceforth dwelling upon these hot aridities, sole solitary lords of Asphaltum.

Doubtless, so quaintly dolorous a thought was originally inspired by the woe-begone landscape itself; but more particularly, perhaps, by the tortoises. For, apart from their strictly physical features, there is something strangely self-condemned in the appearance of these creatures. Lasting sorrow and penal hopelessness are in no animal form so suppliantly expressed as in theirs; while the thought of their wonderful longevity does not fail to enhance the impression.

Nor even at the risk of meriting the charge of absurdly believing in enchantments, can I restrain the admission that sometimes, even now, when leaving the crowded city to wander out July and August among the Adirondack Mountains, far from the influences of towns and proportionally nigh to the mysterious ones of nature; when at such times I sit me down in the mossy head of some deep-wooded gorge, surrounded by prostrate trunks of blasted pines and recall, as in a dream, my other and far-distant rovings in the baked heart of the charmed isles; and remember the sudden glimpses of dusky shells, and long languid necks protruded from the leafless thickets; and again have beheld the vitreous inland rocks worn down and grooved into deep ruts by ages and ages of the slow draggings of tortoises in quest of pools of scanty water; I can hardly resist the feeling that in my time I have indeed slept upon evilly enchanted ground.

Nay, such is the vividness of my memory, or the magic of my fancy, that I know not whether I am not the occasional victim of optical delusion concerning the Gallipagos.

For, often in scenes of social merriment, and especially at revels held by candle-light in old-fashioned mansions, so that shadows are thrown into the further recesses of an angular and spacious room, making them put on a look of haunted undergrowth of lonely woods, I have drawn the attention of my comrades by my fixed gaze and sudden change of air, as I have seemed to see, slowly emerging from those imagined solitudes, and heavily crawling along the floor, the ghost of a gigantic tortoise, with "Memento * * * * *" burning in live letters upon his back.

Two

Now Herman Melville takes up a more specific consideration of the famous Galapagos tortoises. He describes their "vast shells" and their behavior, as well as noting their value to visiting sailors on ships such as the Acushnet cruising the Galapagos Islands looking for sperm whales. Fresh tortoise meat was always a welcome change from salt beef and wormy hardtack.

It was on October 30, 1841 that the future author first sighted the Galapagos Islands as the Acushnet approached Albemarle Island [Isabela]. Here a party landed to capture the tortoises that so enthrall Melville in this sketch.

In spite of his generally gloomy view of the Galapagos Islands, and of the lives he portrays in his writings, for once Melville does take pains in this sketch to point out the "bright" as well as the "dark" side of this creature—a creature that lends itself so well to metaphor.

SKETCH SECOND.
TWO SIDES TO A TORTOISE.

"Most ugly shapes and horrible aspects,
Such as Dame Nature selfe mote feare to see,
Or shame, that ever should so fowle defects
From her most cunning hand escaped bee;
All dreadfull pourtraicts of deformitee.
No wonder if these do a man appall;
For all that here at home we dreadfull hold
Be but as bugs to fearen babes withall
Compared to the creatures in these isles' entrall

"Fear naught, then said the palmer, well avized,
For these same monsters are not there indeed,
But are into these fearful shapes disguized.

"And lifting up his vertuous staffe on high,
Then all that dreadful armie fast gan flye
Into great Zethy's bosom, where they hidden lye."

In view of the description given, may one be gay upon the Encantadas? Yes: that is, find one the gayety, and he will be gay. And, indeed, sackcloth and ashes as they are, the isles are not perhaps unmitigated gloom. For while no spectator can deny their claims to a most solemn and superstitious consideration, no more than my firmest resolutions can decline to behold the spectre-tortoise when emerging from its shadowy recess; yet even the tortoise, dark and melancholy as it is upon the back, still possesses a bright side; its calipee or breast-plate being sometimes of a faint yellowish or golden tinge.

Moreover, every one knows that tortoises as well as turtle are of such a make, that if you but put them on their backs you thereby expose their bright sides without the possibility of their recovering themselves, and turning into view the other. But after you have done this, and because you have done this, you should not swear that the tortoise has no dark side. Enjoy the bright, keep it turned up perpetually if you can, but be honest, and don't deny the black.

Neither should he, who cannot turn the tortoise from its natural position so as to hide the darker and expose his livelier aspect, like a great October pumpkin in the sun, for that cause declare the creature to be one total inky blot. The tortoise is both black and bright. But let us to particulars.

Some months before my first stepping ashore upon the group, my ship was cruising in its close vicinity. One noon we found ourselves off the South Head of Albemarle, and not very far from the land. Partly by way of freak, and partly by way of spying out so strange a country, a boat's crew was sent ashore, with orders to see all they could, and besides, bring back whatever tortoises they could conveniently transport.

It was after sunset, when the adventurers returned. I looked down over the ship's high side as if looking down over the curb of a well, and dimly saw the damp boat, deep in the sea with some un-wonted weight. Ropes were dropt over, and presently three huge antediluvian-looking tortoises, after much straining, were landed on deck. They seemed hardly of the seed of earth.

We had been broad upon the waters for five long months, a period amply sufficient to make all things of the land wear a fabulous hue to the dreamy mind. Had three Spanish custom-house officers boarded us then, it is not unlikely that I should have curiously stared at them, felt of them, and stroked them much as savages serve civilized guests.

But instead of three custom-house officers, behold these really wondrous tortoises—none of your schoolboy mud-turtles—but black as widower's weeds, heavy as chests of plate, with vast shells medallioned and orbed like shields, and dented and blistered like shields that have breasted a battle, shaggy, too, here and there, with dark green moss, and slimy with the spray of the sea.

These mystic creatures, suddenly translated by night from unutterable solitudes to our peopled deck, affected me in a manner not easy to unfold. They seemed newly crawled forth from beneath the foundations of the world. Yea, they seemed the identical tortoises whereon the Hindoo plants this total sphere. With a lantern I inspected them more closely. Such worshipful venerableness of aspect!

Such furry greenness mantling the rude peelings and healing the fissures of their shattered shells. I no more saw three tortoises. They expanded— became transfigured. I seemed to see three Roman Coliseums in magnificent decay.

Ye oldest inhabitants of this, or any other isle, said I, pray, give me the freedom of your three-walled towns.

The great feeling inspired by these creatures was that of age:—dateless, indefinite endurance. And in fact that any other creature can live and breathe as long as the tortoise of the Encantadas, I will not readily believe. Not to hint of their known capacity of sustaining life, while going without food for an entire year, consider that impregnable armor of their living mail. What other bodily being possesses such a citadel wherein to resist the assaults of Time?

As, lantern in hand, I scraped among the moss and beheld the ancient scars of bruises received in many a sullen fall among the marly mountains of the isle—scars strangely widened, swollen, half obliterate, and yet distorted like those sometimes found in the bark of very hoary trees, I seemed an antiquary of a geologist, studying the bird-tracks and ciphers upon the exhumed slates trod by incredible creatures whose very ghosts are now defunct.

As I lay in my hammock that night, overhead I heard the slow weary draggings of the three ponderous strangers along the encumbered deck. Their stupidity or their resolution was so great, that they never went aside for any impediment.

One ceased his movements altogether just before the mid-watch. At sunrise I found him butted like a battering-ram against the immovable foot of the foremast, and still striving, tooth and nail, to force the impossible passage.

That these tortoises are the victims of a penal, or malignant, or perhaps a downright diabolical enchanter, seems in nothing more likely than in that strange infatuation of hopeless toil which so often possesses them. I have known them in their journeyings ram themselves heroically against rocks, and long abide there, nudging, wriggling, wedging, in order to displace them, and so hold on their inflexible path. Their crowning curse is their drudging impulse to straightforwardness in a belittered world.

Meeting with no such hinderance as their companion did, the other tortoises merely fell foul of small stumbling-blocks—buckets, blocks, and coils of rigging—and at times in the act of crawling over them would slip with an astounding rattle to the deck. Listening to these draggings and concussions, I thought me of the haunt from which they came; an isle full of metallic ravines and gulches, sunk bottomlessly into the hearts of splintered mountains, and covered for many miles with inextricable thickets.

I then pictured these three straight-forward monsters, century after century, writhing through the shades, grim as blacksmiths; crawling so slowly and ponderously, that not only did toad-stools and all fungus things grow beneath their feet, but a sooty moss sprouted upon their backs. With them I lost myself in volcanic mazes; brushed away endless boughs of rotting thickets; till finally in a dream I found myself sitting crosslegged upon the foremost, a Brahmin similarly mounted upon either side, forming a tripod of foreheads which upheld the universal cope.

Such was the wild nightmare begot by my first impression of the Encantadas tortoise. But next evening, strange to say, I sat down with my shipmates, and made a merry repast from tortoise steaks, and tortoise stews; and supper over, out knife, and helped convert the three mighty concave shells into three fanciful soup-tureens, and polished the three flat yellowish calipees into three gorgeous salvers.

Three

What an evocative portrait of Galapagos Island birdlife!

Melville here describes the towering promontory of Rock Redondo rising 250 feet out of the sea off the northwest coast of Albemarle Island—today's Isla Isabela.

He skillfully animates the sights and sounds of teeming rookeries, those that today's visitors so often remember as a highlight of their trip.

SKETCH THIRD.
ROCK RODONDO.

"For they this tight the Rock of vile Reproach,
A dangerous and dreadful place,
To which nor fish nor fowl did once approach,
But yelling meaws with sea-gulls hoars and bace
And cormoyrants with birds of ravenous race,
Which still sit waiting on that dreadful clift."

"With that the rolling sea resounding soft
In his big base them fitly answered,
And on the Rock, the waves breaking aloft,
A solemn ineane unto them measured."

"Then he the boteman bad row easily,
And let him heare some part of that rare melody."

"Suddeinly an innumerable flight
Of harmefull fowles about them fluttering cride,
And with their wicked wings them oft did smight
And sore annoyed, groping in that griesly night."

"Even all the nation of unfortunate
And fatal birds about them flocked were."

To go up into a high stone tower is not only a very fine thing in itself, but the very best mode of gaining a comprehensive view of the region round about. It is all the better if this tower stand solitary and alone, like that mysterious Newport one, or else be sole survivor of some perished castle.

Now, with reference to the Enchanted Isles, we are fortunately supplied with just such a noble point of observation in a remarkable rock, from its peculiar figure called of old by the Spaniards, Rock Rodondo, or Round Rock. Some two hundred and fifty feet high, rising straight from the sea ten miles from land, with the whole mountainous group to the south and east. Rock Rodondo occupies, on a large scale, very much the position which the famous Campanile or detached Bell Tower of St. Mark does with respect to the tangled group of hoary edifices around it.

Ere ascending, however, to gaze abroad upon the Encantadas, this sea-tower itself claims attention. It is visible at the distance of thirty miles; and, fully participating in that enchantment which pervades the group, when first seen afar invariably is mistaken for a sail. Four leagues away, of a golden, hazy noon, it seems some Spanish Admiral's ship, stacked up with glittering canvas. Sail ho! Sail ho! Sail ho! from all three masts. But coming nigh, the enchanted frigate is transformed apace into a craggy keep.

My first visit to the spot was made in the gray of the morning. With a view of fishing, we had lowered three boats and pulling some two miles from our vessel, found ourselves just before dawn of day close under the moon-shadow of Rodondo. Its aspect was heightened, and yet softened, by the strange double twilight of the hour. The great full moon burnt in the low west like a half-spent beacon, casting a soft mellow tinge upon the sea like that cast by a waning fire of embers upon a midnight hearth; while along the entire east the invisible sun sent pallid intimations of his coming.

The wind was light; the waves languid; the stars twinkled with a faint effulgence; all nature seemed supine with the long night watch, and half-suspended in jaded expectation of the sun. This was the critical hour to catch Rodondo in his perfect mood. The twilight was just enough to reveal every striking point, without tearing away the dim investiture of wonder.

From a broken stair-like base, washed, as the steps of a water-palace, by the waves, the tower rose in entablatures of strata to a shaven summit. These uniform layers, which compose the mass, form its most peculiar feature. For at their lines of junction they project flatly into encircling shelves, from top to bottom, rising one above another in graduated series. And as the eaves of any old barn or abbey are alive with swallows, so were all these rocky ledges with unnumbered sea-fowl. Eaves upon eaves, and nests upon nests. Here and there were long birdlime streaks of a ghostly white staining the tower from sea to air, readily accounting for its sail-like look afar.

All would have been bewitchingly quiescent, were it not for the demoniac din created by the birds. Not only were the eaves rustling with them, but they flew densely overhead, spreading themselves into a winged and continually shifting canopy. The tower is the resort of aquatic birds for hundreds of leagues around. To the north, to the east, to the west, stretches nothing but eternal ocean; so that the man-of-war hawk coming from the coasts of North America, Polynesia, or Peru, makes his first land at Rodondo.

And yet though Rodondo be terra-firma, no land-bird ever lighted on it. Fancy a red-robin or a canary there! What a falling into the hands of the Philistines, when the poor warbler should be surrounded by such locust-flights of strong bandit birds, with long bills cruel as daggers.

I know not where one can better study the Natural History of strange sea-fowl than at Rodondo. It is the aviary of Ocean. Birds light here which never touched mast or tree; hermit-birds, which ever fly alone; cloud-birds, familiar with un-pierced zones of air.

Let us first glance low down to the lower-most shelf of all, which is the widest, too, and but a little space from high-water mark. What outlandish beings are these? Erect as men, but hardly as symmetrical, they stand all round the rock like sculptured caryatides, supporting the next range of eaves above. Their bodies are grotesquely misshapen; their bills short; their feet seemingly legless; while the members at their sides are neither fin, wing, nor arm. And truly neither fish, flesh, nor fowl is the penguin; as an edible, pertaining neither to Carnival nor Lent; without exception

the most ambiguous and least lovely creature yet discovered by man.

Though dabbling in all three elements, and indeed possessing some rudimental claims to all, the penguin is at home in none. On land it stumps; afloat it sculls; in the air it flops. As if ashamed of her failure, Nature keeps this ungainly child hidden away at the ends of the earth, in the Straits of Magellan, and on the abased sea-story of Rodondo.

But look, what are yon wobegone regiments drawn up on the next shelf above? what rank and file of large strange fowl? what sea Friars of Orders Gray? Pelicans. Their elongated bills, and heavy leathern pouches suspended thereto, give them the most lugubrious expression. A pensive race, they stand for hours together without motion. Their dull, ashy plumage imparts an aspect as if they had been powdered over with cinders. A penitential bird, indeed, fitly haunting the shores of the clinkered Encantadas, whereon tormented Job himself might have well sat down and scraped himself with potsherds.

Higher up now we mark the gony, or gray albatross, anomalously so called, an unsightly unpoetic bird, unlike its storied kinsman, which is the snow-white ghost of the haunted Capes of Hope and Horn.

As we still ascend from shelf to shelf, we find the tenants of the tower serially disposed in order of their magnitude:—gannets, black and speckled haglets,

jays, sea-hens, sperm-whale-birds, gulls of all varie-
ties:—thrones, princedoms, powers, dominating
one above another in senatorial array; while, sprin-
kled over all, like an ever-repeated fly in a great
piece of broidery, the stormy petrel or Mother
Cary's chicken sounds his continual challenge and
alarm. That this mysterious hummingbird of
ocean—which, had it but brilliancy of hue, might,
from its evanescent liveliness, be almost called its
butterfly, yet whose chirrup under the stern is omi-
nous to mariners as to the peasant the death-tick
sounding from behind the chimney jamb—should
have its special haunt at the Encantadas, contrib-
utes, in the seaman's mind, not a little to their
dreary spell.

As day advances the dissonant din aug-
ments. With ear-splitting cries the wild birds cele-
brate their matins. Each moment, flights push from
the tower, and join the aerial choir hovering overhead, while their places below are supplied by dart-
ing myriads. But down through all this discord of
commotion, I hear clear, silver, bugle-like notes
unbrokenly falling, like oblique lines of swift-
slanting rain in a cascading shower. I gaze far up,
and behold a snow-white angelic thing, with one
long, lance-like feather thrust out behind. It is the
bright, inspiriting chanticleer of ocean, the beaute-
ous bird, from its bestirring whistle of musical in-
vocation, fitly styled the "Boatswain's Mate."

The winged, life-clouding Rodondo had its
full counterpart in the finny hosts which peopled
the waters at its base. Below the water-line, the rock
seemed one honey-comb of grottoes, affording
labyrinthine lurking-places for swarms of fairy fish.
All were strange; many exceedingly beautiful; and
would have well graced the costliest glass globes in

which gold-fish are kept for a show. Nothing was more striking than the complete novelty of many individuals of this multitude. Here hues were seen as yet unpainted, and figures which are unengraved.

To show the multitude, avidity, and nameless fearlessness and tameness of these fish, let me say, that often, marking through clear spaces of water—temporarily made so by the concentric dartings of the fish above the surface—certain larger and less unwary wights, which swam slow and deep; our anglers would cautiously essay to drop their lines down to these last. But in vain; there was no passing the uppermost zone. No sooner did the hook touch the sea, than a hundred infatuates contended for the honor of capture. Poor fish of Rodondo! in your victimized confidence, you are of the number of those who inconsiderately trust, while they do not understand, human nature.

But the dawn is now fairly day. Band after band, the sea-fowl sail away to forage the deep for their food. The tower is left solitary save the fish-caves at its base. Its birdlime gleams in the golden rays like the whitewash of a tall light-house, or the lofty sails of a cruiser. This moment, doubtless, while we know it to be a dead desert rock other voyagers are taking oaths it is a glad populous ship.

But ropes now, and let us ascend. Yet soft, this is not so easy.

Four

In this sketch Melville uses his imagined climb (for this rock is not so easily scalable) to give the reader an introduction to island geography. He situates the archipelago in relation to other land masses in the Southern Hemisphere and then describes four of its islands in detail (Albemarle [Isabela], Narborough [Fernandina], Abington [Pinta], and James's [San Salvador/Santiago]) as well as noting several others.

"Pisgah" in the title refers to the Biblical mountain beside the Dead Sea from which the Lord first showed Moses the Promised Land.

The gathering of ships he describes encountering in Weather and Lee Bays was based—with slight exaggeration—on a group of four American whalers, including the Acushnet, hunting these rich calving grounds on November 2, 1841.

The Cowley he mentions was buccaneer Captain William Ambrosia Cowley who named and charted many of these islands in the late 1600s.

Melville relied on Captain Cowley's Voyage Round the Globe, published in 1699, as one source of information about the Galapagos Islands.

Another of his sources was Charles Darwin's Zoology of the Voyage of the H.M.S. Beagle, published in 1839 as one portion of Captain Robert Fitz-Roy's four volume Narrative of the Surveying Voyages of His Majesty's Ships Adventure and Beagle. Perhaps it is this narrative that leads to one of Melville's rare touches of humor: the parody in this sketch of a naturalist's listing of an island's inhabitants.

SKETCH FOURTH.
A PISGAH VIEW FROM THE ROCK.

*—"That done, he leads him to the highest
   mount,
From whence, far off he unto him did show:"—*

If you seek to ascend Rock Rodondo, take
the following prescription. Go three voyages round
the world as a main-royal-man of the tallest frigate
that floats; then serve a year or two apprenticeship
to the guides who conduct strangers up the Peak of
Teneriffe; and as many more respectively to a rope-
dancer, an Indian juggler, and a chamois. This
done, come and be rewarded by the view from our
tower.

How we get there, we alone know. If we
sought to tell others, what the wiser were they? Suffice it, that here at the summit you and I stand.
Does any balloonist, does the outlooking man in the
moon, take a broader view of space? Much thus,
one fancies, looks the universe from Milton's celes-
tial battlements. A boundless watery Kentucky.
Here Daniel Boone would have dwelt content.

Never heed for the present yonder Burnt
District of the Enchanted Isles. Look edgeways, as it
were, past them, to the south. You see nothing; but
permit me to point out the direction, if not the
place, of certain interesting objects in the vast sea,
which, kissing this tower's base, we behold un-
scrolling itself towards the Antarctic Pole.

We stand now ten miles from the Equator.
Yonder, to the East, some six hundred miles, lies

the continent; this Rock being just about on the parallel of Quito.

Observe another thing here. We are at one of three uninhabited clusters, which, at pretty nearly uniform distances from the main, sentinel, at long intervals from each other, the entire coast of South America. In a peculiar manner, also, they terminate the South American character of country. Of the unnumbered Polynesian chains to the westward, not one partakes of the qualities of the Encantadas or Gallipagos, the isles of St. Felix and St. Ambrose, the isles Juan-Fernandez and Massafuero.

Of the first, it needs not here to speak. The second lie a little above the Southern Tropic; lofty, inhospitable, and uninhabitable rocks, one of which, presenting two round hummocks connected by a low reef, exactly resembles a huge double-headed shot. The last lie in the latitude of 33°; high, wild and cloven.

Juan Fernandez is sufficiently famous without further description.

Massafuero is a Spanish name, expressive of the fact, that the isle so called lies *more without*, that is, further off the main than its neighbor Juan. This isle Massafuero has a very imposing aspect at a distance of eight or ten miles. Approached in one direction, in cloudy weather, its great overhanging height and rugged contour, and more especially a peculiar slope of its broad summits, give it much the air of a vast iceberg drifting in tremendous poise. Its sides are split with dark cavernous recesses, as an old cathedral with its gloomy lateral chapels. Drawing nigh one of these gorges from sea, after a long voyage, and beholding some tatter demalion outlaw, staff in hand, descending its steep rocks toward you, conveys a very queer emotion to a lover of the picturesque.

On fishing parties from ships, at various times, I have chanced to visit each of these groups. The impression they give to the stranger pulling close up in his boat under their grim cliffs is, that surely he must be their first discoverer, such, for the most part, is the unimpaired ... silence and solitude. And here, by the way, the mode in which these isles were really first lighted upon by Europeans is not unworthy of mention, especially as what is about to be said, likewise applies to the original discovery of our Encantadas.

Prior to the year 1563, the voyages made by Spanish ships from Peru to Chili, were full of difficulty. Along this coast, the winds from the South most generally prevail; and it had been an invariable custom to keep close in with the land, from a superstitious conceit on the part of the Spaniards, that were they to lose sight of it, the eternal tradewind would waft them into unending waters, from whence would be no return. Here, involved among tortuous capes and headlands, shoals and reefs, beating, too, against a continual head wind, often light, and sometimes for days and weeks sunk into utter calm, the provincial vessels, in many cases, suffered the extremest hardships, in passages, which at the present day seem to have been incredibly protracted.

There is on record in some collections of nautical disasters, an account of one of these ships, which, starting on a voyage whose duration was estimated at ten days, spent four months at sea, and indeed never again entered harbor, for in the end she was cast away. Singular to tell, this craft never encountered a gale, but was the vexed sport of malicious calms and currents. Thrice, out of provisions, she put back to an intermediate port, and started afresh, but only yet again to return. Frequent fogs enveloped her; so that no observation could be had of her place, and once, when all hands were joyously anticipating sight of their destination, lo! the vapors lifted and disclosed the mountains from which they had taken their first departure. In the like deceptive vapors she at last struck upon a reef, whence ensued a long series of calamities too sad to detail.

It was the famous pilot, Juan Fernandez, immortalized by the island named after him, who put an end to these coasting tribulations, by boldly venturing the experiment—as De Gama did before him with respect to Europe—of standing broad out from land. Here he found the winds favorable for getting to the South, and by running westward till beyond the influences of the trades, he regained the coast without difficulty; making the passage which, though in a high degree circuitous, proved far more expeditious than the nominally direct one.

Now it was upon these new tracks, and about the year 1670, or thereabouts, that the Enchanted Isles, and the rest of the sentinel groups, as they may be called, were discovered. Though I know of no account as to whether any of them were found inhabited or no, it may be reasonably concluded that they have been immemorial solitudes. But let us return to Redondo.

Southwest from our tower lies all Polynesia, hundreds of leagues away; but straight west, on the precise line of his parallel, no land rises till your keel is beached upon the Kingsmills, a nice little sail of, say 5000 miles.

Having thus by such distant references—with Rodondo the only possible ones—settled our relative place on the sea, let us consider objects not quite so remote.

Behold the grim and charred Enchanted Isles. This nearest crater-shaped headland is part of Albemarle [Isabela], the largest of the group, being some sixty miles or more long, and fifteen broad.

Did you ever lay eye on the real genuine Equator? Have you ever, in the largest sense, toed the Line? Well, that identical crater-shaped headland there, all yellow lava, is cut by the Equator exactly as a knife cuts straight through the centre of a pumpkin pie.

If you could only see so far, just to one side of that same headland, across yon low dikey ground, you would catch sight of the isle of Narborough [Fernandina], the loftiest land of the cluster; no soil whatever; one seamed clinker from top to bottom; abounding in black caves like smithies; its metallic shore ringing under foot like plates of iron; its central volcanoes standing grouped like a gigantic chimney-stack.

Narborough [Fernandina] and Albemarle [Isabela] are neighbors after a quite curious fashion. A familiar diagram will illustrate this strange neighborhood:

Ⅎ

Cut a channel at the above letter joint, and the middle transverse limb is Narborough [Fernandina], and all the rest is Albemarle [Isabela]. Volcanic Narborough [Fernandina] lies in the black jaws of Albemarle [Isabela] like a wolf's red tongue in his open month.

If now you desire the population of Albemarle [Isabela], I will give you, in round numbers, the statistics, according to the most reliable estimates made upon the spot:

Men,	none
Ant-eaters,	unknown
Man-haters,	unknown
Lizards,	500,000
Snakes,	500,000
Spiders,	10,000,000
Salamanders,	unknown
Devils,	ditto

Making a clean total of: 11,000,000

exclusive of an incomputable host of fiends, ant-eaters, man-haters, and salamanders.

Albemarle [Isabela] opens his mouth towards the setting sun. His distended jaws form a great bay, which Narborough [Fernandina], his tongue, divides into halves, one whereof is called Weather Bay, the other Lee Bay; while the volcanic promontories, terminating his coasts, are styled South Head and North Head.

I note this, because these bays are famous in the annals of the Sperm Whale Fishery. The whales come here at certain seasons to calve. When ships first cruised hereabouts, I am told, they used to blockade the entrance of Lee Bay, when their boats going round by Weather Bay, passed through Narborough [Fernandina] channel, and so had the Leviathans very neatly in a pen.

The day after we took fish at the base of this Round Tower, we had a fine wind, and shooting round the north headland, suddenly descried a fleet of full thirty sail, all beating to windward like a squadron in line. A brave sight as ever man saw. A most harmonious concord of rushing keels. Their thirty kelsons hummed like thirty harp-strings, and looked as straight whilst they left their parallel traces on the sea.

But there proved too many hunters for the game. The fleet broke up, and went their separate ways out of sight, leaving my own ship and two trim gentlemen of London. These last, finding no luck either, likewise vanished; and Lee Bay, with all its appurtenances, and without a rival, devolved to us.

The way of cruising here is this. You keep hovering about the entrance of the bay, in one beat and out the next. But at times—not always, as in other parts of the group—a racehorse of a current sweeps right across its mouth. So, with all sails set, you carefully ply your tacks. How often, standing at the foremast head at sunrise, with our patient prow pointed in between these isles, did I gaze upon that land, not of cakes, but of clinkers, not of streams of sparkling water, but arrested torrents of tormented lava.

As the ship runs in from the open sea, Narborough [Fernandina] presents its side in one dark craggy mass, soaring up some five or six thousand feet, at which point it hoods itself in heavy clouds, whose lowest level fold is as clearly defined against the rocks as the snow-line against the Andes.

There is dire mischief going on in that upper dark. There toil the demons of fire, who, at intervals, irradiate the nights with a strange spectral illumination for miles and miles around, but unaccompanied by any further demonstration; or else, suddenly announce themselves by terrific concussions, and the full drama of a volcanic eruption. The blacker that cloud by day, the more may you look for light by night. Often whalemen have found themselves cruising nigh that burning mountain when all aglow with a ball-room blaze. Or, rather, glass-works, you may call this same vitreous isle of Narborough [Fernandina], with its tall chimney-stacks.

Where we still stand, here on Rodondo, we cannot see all the other isles, but it is a good place from which to point out where they lie. Yonder, though, to the E.N.E., I mark a distant dusky ridge. It is Abington Isle [Pinta], one of the most northerly of the group; so solitary, remote, and blank, it looks like No-Man's Land seen off our northern shore. I doubt whether two human beings ever touched upon that spot. So far as yon Abington Isle [Pinta] is concerned, Adam and his billions of posterity remain uncreated.

Ranging south of Abington [Pinta], and quite out of sight behind the long spine of Albemarle, lies James's Isle [San Salvador/Santiago], so called by the early Buccaneers after the luckless Stuart, Duke of York.

Observe here, by the way, that, excepting the isles particularized in comparatively recent times, and which mostly received the names of famous Admirals, the Encantadas were first christened by the Spaniards; but these Spanish names were generally effaced on English charts by the subsequent christenings of the Buccaneers, who, in the middle of the seventeenth century, called them after English noblemen and kings.

Of these loyal freebooters and the things which associate their name with the Encantadas, we shall hear anon. Nay, for one little item, immediately; for between James's Isle [San Salvador/Santiago] and Albemarle [Isabela], lies a fantastic islet, strangely known as "Cowley's Enchanted Isle [Cowley]." But, as all the group is deemed enchanted, the reason must be given for the spell within a spell involved by this particular designation.

The name was bestowed by that excellent Buccaneer himself, on his first visit here. Speaking in his published voyages of this spot, he says—"My fancy led me to call it Cowley's Enchanted Isle, for, we having had a sight of it upon several points of the compass, it appeared always in so many different forms; sometimes like a ruined fortification; upon another point like a great city," etc. No wonder though, that among the Encantadas all sorts of ocular deceptions and mirages should be met.

That Cowley linked his name with this self-transforming and bemocking isle, suggests the possibility that it conveyed to him some meditative image of himself. At least, as is not impossible, if he were any relative of the mildly-thoughtful and self-upbraiding poet Cowley, who lived about his time, the conceit might seem unwarranted; for that sort of thing evinced in the naming of this isle runs in the blood, and may be seen in pirates as in poets.

Still south of James's Isle [San Salvador/Santiago] lie Jervis Isle [Rabida], Duncan Isle [Pinzon], Crossman's Isle [several possible islets], Brattle Isle [Tortuga], Wood's Isle [Santa Maria / Floreana], Chatham Isle [San Cristobal], and various lesser isles, for the most part an archipelago of aridities, without inhabitant, history, or hope of either in all time to come.

But not far from these are rather notable isles—Barrington [Santa Fe], Charles's [Santa Maria/Floreana], Norfolk [Santa Cruz], and Hood's [Espanola]. Succeeding chapters will reveal some ground for their notability.

Five

After four sketches depicting the natural history of the archipelago, Melville now begins to give some indication of its human history.

In this, the shortest of his sketches, he recounts one episode among the heroic feats of Captain David Porter and the USS Essex during the War of 1812. Melville used Porter's Journal of a Cruise Made to the Pacific Ocean, published in 1815, as a source here and in many of his other writings about the South Pacific.

The 32-gun frigate Essex, built in Salem, Massachusetts as the first of five Navy warships of the same name, joined the fledgling US Navy in 1799. Although she fought against several foes including the Barbary pirates, her exploits in the War of 1812 were most famous.

Under Captain Porter the Essex captured numerous British ships and severely disrupted British whale fisheries in the South Pacific. One story claims Captain Porter cleverly used information from letters in the Post Office barrel on Charles's Island [Santa Maria/Floreana] to target many of the 30 or more British ships captured in Galapagos waters.

In March 1814, after losing half her crew in an intense sea battle near Valparaiso, Chile, she was captured by a British warship and pressed into Royal Navy service as the HMS Essex until 1837.

Interestingly, an American whaling ship also named the Essex was attacked and sunk by a sperm whale in the South Pacific in 1820, partially inspiring Melville's story of Moby-Dick.

SKETCH FIFTH.
THE FRIGATE, AND SHIP FLYAWAY.

"Looking far forth into the ocean wide,
A goodly ship with banners bravely dight,
And flag in her top-gallant I espide,
Through the main sea making her merry flight."

Ere quitting Rodondo, it must not be omitted that here, in 1813, the U.S. frigate *Essex*, Captain David Porter, came near leaving her bones.

Lying becalmed one morning with a strong current setting her rapidly towards the rock, a strange sail was descried, which—not out of keeping with alleged enchantments of the neighborhood—seemed to be staggering under a violent wind, while the frigate lay lifeless as if spell-bound.

But a light air springing up, all sail was made by the frigate in chase of the enemy, as supposed—he being deemed an English whale-ship—but the rapidity of the current was so great, that soon all sight was lost of him; and, at meridian, the *Essex*, spite of her drags, was driven so close under the foam-lashed cliffs of Rodondo that, for a time, all hands gave her up.

A smart breeze, however, at last helped her off, though the escape was so critical as to seem almost miraculous.

Thus saved from destruction herself, she now made use of that salvation to destroy the other vessel, if possible. Renewing the chase in the direction in which the stranger had disappeared, sight was caught of him the following morning. Upon being descried he hoisted American colors and stood away from the *Essex*.

A calm ensued; when, still confident that the stranger was an Englishman, Porter dispatched a cutter, not to board the enemy, but drive back his boats engaged in towing him. The cutter succeeded. Cutters were subsequently sent to capture him; the stranger now showing English colors in place of American. But, when the frigate's boats were within a short distance of their hoped-for prize, another sudden breeze sprang up; the stranger, under all sail, bore off to the westward, and, ere night, was hull down ahead of the *Essex*, which, all this time, lay perfectly becalmed.

This enigmatic craft—American in the morning, and English in the evening—her sails full

of wind in a calm—was never again beheld. An enchanted ship no doubt. So, at least, the sailors
swore.

This cruise of the *Essex* in the Pacific during
the war of 1812, is, perhaps, the strangest and most
stirring to be found in the history of the American
navy. She captured the furthest wandering vessels;
visited the remotest seas and isles; long hovered in
the charmed vicinity of the enchanted group; and,
finally, valiantly gave up the ghost fighting two
English frigates in the harbor of Valparaiso.

Mention is made of her here for the same
reason that the Buccaneers will likewise receive record; because, like them, by long cruising among
the isles, tortoise-hunting upon their shores, and
generally exploring them; for these and other rea-
sons, the *Essex* is peculiarly associated with the Encantadas.

Here be it said that you have but three, eye-
witness authorities worth mentioning touching the
Enchanted Isles:—Cowley, the Buccaneer (1684);
Colnet the whaling-ground explorer (1798); Porter,
the post captain (1813). Other than these you have
but barren, bootless allusions from some few passing voyagers or compilers.

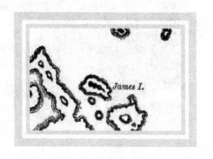

Six

Although Melville set this sketch on Barrington Island [Santa Fe], he was clearly referring to James's Island [San Salvador/Santiago]. Why the change of setting? a mistake? faulty memory? a literary device? No one knows.

Buccaneers William Dampier (English, 1651-1715), Lionel Wafer (Welsh, 1640-1705), and the previously mentioned William Ambrosia Cowley (English, ?-?) named by Melville in this sketch were famous early visitors to the Galapagos Islands. All three sailed with a pirate fleet roaming the archipelago in the 1680s. And all three returned to England to write about their adventures while avoiding the fate of many of their contemporaries: execution for piracy.

SKETCH SIXTH.
BARRINGTON ISLE AND THE BUCCANEERS.

"Let us all servile base subjection scorn,
And as we be sons of the earth so wide,
Let us our father's heritage divide,
And challenge to ourselves our portions dew
Of all the patrimony, which a few
hold on hugger-mugger in their hand."

"Lords of the world, and so will wander free,
Whereso us listeth, uncontroll'd of any."

"How bravely now we live, how jocund, how near
The first inheritance, without fear, how free from
little troubles!"

Near two centuries ago Barrington Isle [Santa Fe] was the resort of that famous wing of the West Indian Buccaneers, which, upon their repulse from the Cuban waters, crossing the Isthmus of Darien, ravaged the Pacific side of the Spanish colonies, and, with the regularity and timing of a modern mail, waylaid the royal treasure-ships plying between Manilla and Acapulco. After the toils of piratic war, here they came to say their prayers, enjoy their free-and-easies, count their crackers from the cask, their doubloons from the keg, and measure their silks of Asia with long Toledos [swords] for their yard-sticks.

As a secure retreat, an undiscoverable hiding-place, no spot in those days could have been better fitted. In the centre of a vast and silent sea, but very little traversed—surrounded by islands, whose inhospitable aspect might well drive away the chance navigator—and yet within a few days' sail of the opulent countries which they made their prey—the unmolested Buccaneers found here that tranquillity which they fiercely denied to every civilized harbor in that part of the world.

Here, after stress of weather, or a temporary drubbing at the hands of their vindictive foes, or in swift flight with golden booty, those old marauders came, and lay snugly out of all harm's reach. But not only was the place a harbor of safety, and a bower of ease, but for utility in other things it was most admirable.

Barrington Isle [Santa Fe] is, in many respects, singularly adapted to careening, refitting, refreshing, and other seamen's purposes. Not only has it good water, and good anchorage, well

sheltered from all winds by the high land of Albemarle, but it is the least unproductive isle of the
group. Tortoises good for food, trees good for fuel,
and long grass good for bedding, abound here, and
there are pretty natural walks, and several landscapes to be seen. Indeed, though in its locality be-
longing to the Enchanted group, Barrington Isle
[Santa Fe] is so unlike most of its neighbors, that it
would hardly seem of kin to them.

"I once landed on its western side," says a
sentimental voyager long ago, "where it faces the
black buttress of Albemarle [Isabela]. I walked beneath groves of trees—not very lofty, and not palm
trees, or orange trees, or peach trees, to be sure—
but, for all that, after long sea-faring, very beautiful
to walk under, even though they supplied no fruit.

"And here, in calm spaces at the heads of
glades, and on the shaded tops of slopes command-
ing the most quiet scenery—what do you think I
saw? Seats which might have served Brahmins and

presidents of peace societies. Fine old ruins of what had once been symmetric lounges of stone and turf, they bore every mark both of artificialness and age, and were, undoubtedly, made by the Buccaneers. One had been a long sofa, with back and arms, just such a sofa as the poet Gray might have loved to throw himself upon, his Crebillon in hand.

"Though they sometimes tarried here for months at a time, and used the spot for a storing-place for spare spars, sails, and casks; yet it is highly improbable that the Buccaneers ever erected dwelling-houses upon the isle. They never were here except their ships remained, and they would most likely have slept on board. I mention this, because I cannot avoid the thought, that it is hard to impute the construction of these romantic seats to any other motive than one of pure peacefulness and kindly fellowship with nature.

"That the Buccaneers perpetrated the greatest outrages is very true—that some of them were mere cutthroats is not to be denied; but we know that here and there among their host was a Dampier, a Wafer, and a Cowley, and likewise other men, whose worst reproach was their desperate fortunes—whom persecution, or adversity, or secret and unavengeable wrongs, had driven from Christian society to seek the melancholy solitude or the guilty adventures of the sea. At any rate, long as those ruins of seats on Barrington [Santa Fe] remain, the most singular monuments are furnished to the fact, that all of the Buccaneers were not unmitigated monsters.

"But during my ramble on the isle I was not long in discovering other tokens, of things quite in accordance with those wild traits, popularly, and no doubt truly enough, imputed to the freebooters at large. Had I picked up old sails and rusty hoops I would only have thought of the ship's carpenter and cooper. But I found old cutlasses and daggers reduced to mere threads of rust, which, doubtless, had stuck between Spanish ribs ere now. These were signs of the murderer and robber; the reveler likewise had left his trace. Mixed with shells, fragments of broken jars were lying here and there, high up upon the beach. They were precisely like the jars now used upon the Spanish coast for the wine and Pisco spirits of that country.

"With a rusty dagger-fragment in one hand, and a bit of a wine-jar in another, I sat me down on the ruinous green sofa I have spoken of, and bethought me long and deeply of these same Buccaneers. Could it be possible, that they robbed and murdered one day, reveled the next, and rested themselves by turning meditative philosophers, rural poets, and seat-builders on the third?

"Not very improbable, after all. For consider the vacillations of a man. Still, strange as it may seem, I must also abide by the more charitable thought; namely, that among these adventurers were some gentlemanly, companionable souls, capable of genuine tranquillity and virtue."

Seven

Melville based the narrative in this sketch loosely—very loosely—upon the history of a Charles's Island [Santa Maria/Floreana] settlement. He conflates the stories of the colony's first two leaders, but after all, these sketches were sold as fiction.

In reality, General Jose Villamil, a hero in Ecuador's (not Peru's) struggle for independence from Spain, founded the first colony in 1832. Eighty mutinous soldiers given the choice of death or settling on the island chose to become colonists. Efforts to establish agricultural or mining enterprises were only minimally successful and over the years, increasingly criminal elements joined the settlement.

Although Villamil governed well, he eventually tired of the struggle and left the island. Colonel Jose Williams then took over and enforced despotic rules with packs of vicious dogs. In 1841, like Melville's Dog-King, he fled for his life during a revolt.

In this sketch Melville's themes of imperialism's evils and the abuse of power often addressed in his earlier novels emerge again.

SKETCH SEVENTH.
CHARLES'S ISLE AND THE DOG-KING.

—So with outragious cry,
A thousand villeins round about him swarmed
Out of the rocks and caves adjoining nye;
Vile caitive wretches, ragged, rude, deformed;
All threatning death, all in straunge manner armed;
Some with unweldy clubs, some with long speares,
Some rusty knives, some staves in fier warmd.

We will not be of any occupation,
Let such vile vassals, born to base vocation,
Drudge in the world, and for their living droyle,
Which have no wit to live withouten toyle.

Southwest of Barrington [Santa Fe] lies Charles's Isle [Santa Maria/Floreana]. And hereby hangs a history which I gathered long ago from a shipmate learned in all the lore of outlandish life.

During the successful revolt of the Spanish provinces from Old Spain, there fought on behalf of Peru a certain Creole adventurer from Cuba, who, by his bravery and good fortune, at length advanced himself to high rank in the patriot army.

The war being ended, Peru found itself like many valorous gentlemen, free and independent enough, but with few shot in the locker. In other words, Peru had not wherewithal to pay off its troops. But the Creole—I forget his name— volunteered to take his pay in lands. So they told him he might have his pick of the Enchanted Isles, which were then, as they still remain, the nominal appanage of Peru.

75

The soldier straightway embarks thither, explores the group, returns to Callao, and says he will take a deed of Charles's Isle [Santa Maria/ Floreana]. Moreover, this deed must stipulate that thenceforth Charles's Isle [Santa Maria/Floreana] is not only the sole property of the Creole, but is forever free of Peru, even as Peru of Spain.

To be short, this adventurer procures himself to be made in effect Supreme Lord of the Island, one of the princes of the powers of the earth.*

*The American Spaniards have long been in the habit of making presents of islands to deserving individuals. The pilot Juan Fernandez procured a deed of the isle named after him, and for some years resided there before Selkirk came. It is supposed, however, that he eventually contracted the blues upon his princely property, for after a time he returned to the main, and as report goes, became a very garrulous barber in the city of Lima.

He now sends forth a proclamation inviting subjects to his as yet unpopulated kingdom. Some eighty souls, men and women, respond; and being provided by their leader with necessaries, and tools of various sorts, together with a few cattle and goats, take ship for the promised land; the last arrival on board, prior to sailing, being the Creole himself, accompanied, strange to say, by a disciplined cavalry company of large grim dogs.

These, it was observed on the passage, refusing to consort with the emigrants, remained aristocratically grouped around their master on the elevated quarter-deck, casting disdainful glances forward upon the inferior rabble there; much as, from the ramparts, the soldiers of a garrison, thrown into a conquered town, eye the inglorious citizen-mob over which they are set to watch.

Now Charles's [Isle Santa Maria/Floreana] not only resembles Barrington Isle [Santa Fe] in being much more inhabitable than other parts of the group, but it is double the size of Barrington [Santa Fe], say forty or fifty miles in circuit.

Safely debarked at last, the company, under direction of their lord and patron, forthwith proceeded to build their capital city. They make considerable advance in the way of walls of clinkers, and lava floors, nicely sanded with cinders.

On the least barren hills they pasture their cattle, while the goats, adventurers by nature, explore the far inland solitudes for a scanty livelihood of lofty herbage. Meantime, abundance of fish and tortoises supply their other wants.

The disorders incident to settling all primitive regions, in the present case were heightened by the peculiarly untoward character of many of the pilgrims. His Majesty was forced at last to proclaim martial law, and actually hunted and shot with his own hand several of his rebellious subjects, who, with most questionable intentions, had clandestinely encamped in the interior, whence they stole by night, to prowl barefooted on tiptoe round the precincts of the lava-palace.

It is to be remarked, however, that prior to such stern proceedings, the more reliable men had been judiciously picked out for an infantry body-guard, subordinate to the cavalry body-guard of dogs. But the state of politics in this unhappy nation may be somewhat imagined, from the circumstance that all who were not of the body-guard were downright plotters and malignant traitors.

At length the death penalty was tacitly abolished, owing to the timely thought, that were strict sportsman's justice to be dispensed among such subjects, ere long the Nimrod King would have little or no remaining game to shoot.

The human part of the life-guard was now disbanded, and set to work cultivating the soil, and raising potatoes; the regular army now solely consisting of the dog-regiment. These, as I have heard, were of a singularly ferocious character, though by severe training rendered docile to their master. Armed to the teeth, the Creole now goes in state, surrounded by his canine janizaries, whose terrific bayings prove quite as serviceable as bayonets in keeping down the surgings of revolt.

But the census of the isle, sadly lessened by the dispensation of justice, and not materially recruited by matrimony, began to fill his mind with sad mistrust. Some way the population must be increased.

Now, from its possessing a little water, and its comparative pleasantness of aspect, Charles's Isle [Santa Maria/Floreana] at this period was occasionally visited by foreign whalers. These His Majesty had always levied upon for port charges, thereby contributing to his revenue.

But now he had additional designs. By insidious arts he, from time to time, cajoles certain sailors to desert their ships, and enlist beneath his banner. Soon as missed, their captains crave permission to go and hunt them up. Whereupon His Majesty first hides them very carefully away, and then freely permits the search. In consequence, the delinquents are never found, and the ships retire without them.

Thus, by a two-edged policy of this crafty monarch, foreign nations were crippled in the number of their subjects, and his own were greatly multiplied. He particularly petted these renegado strangers. But alas for the deep-laid schemes of ambitious princes, and alas for the vanity of glory.

As the foreign-born Pretorians, unwisely introduced into the Roman state, and still more unwisely made favorites of the Emperors, at last insulted and overturned the throne, even so these lawless mariners, with all the rest of the body-guard and all the populace, broke out into a terrible mutiny, and defied their master. He marched against them with all his dogs.

A deadly battle ensued upon the beach. It raged for three hours, the dogs fighting with determined valor, and the sailors reckless of everything but victory. Three men and thirteen dogs were left dead upon the field, many on both sides were wounded, and the king was forced to fly with the remainder of his canine regiment. The enemy pursued, stoning the dogs with their master into the wilderness of the interior.

Discontinuing the pursuit, the victors returned to the village on the shore, stove the spirit casks, and proclaimed a Republic. The dead men were interred with the honors of war, and the dead dogs ignominiously thrown into the sea.

At last, forced by stress of suffering, the fugitive Creole came down from the hills and offered to treat for peace. But the rebels refused it on any other terms than his unconditional banishment. Accordingly, the next ship that arrived carried away the ex-king to Peru.

The history of the king of Charles's Island [Santa Maria/Floreana] furnishes another illustration of the difficulty of colonizing barren islands with unprincipled pilgrims.

Doubtless for a long time the exiled monarch, pensively ruralizing in Peru, which afforded him a safe asylum in his calamity, watched every arrival from the Encantadas, to hear news of the failure of the Republic, the consequent penitence of the rebels, and his own recall to royalty. Doubtless he deemed the Republic but a miserable experiment which would soon explode.

But no, the insurgents had confederated themselves into a democracy neither Grecian, Roman, nor American. Nay, it was no democracy at all, but a permanent *Riotocracy*, which gloried in having no law but lawlessness.

Great inducements being offered to deserters, their ranks were swelled by accessions of scamps from every ship which touched their shores. Charles's Island [Santa Maria/Floreana] was proclaimed the asylum of the oppressed of all navies. Each runaway tar was hailed as a martyr in the cause of freedom, and became immediately installed a ragged citizen of this universal nation.

In vain the captains of absconding seamen strove to regain them. Their new compatriots were ready to give any number of ornamental eyes in their behalf. They had few cannon, but their fists were not to be trifled with.

So at last it came to pass that no vessels acquainted with the character of that country durst touch there, however sorely in want of refreshment. It became Anathema—a sea Alsatia—the unassailed lurking-place of all sorts of desperadoes, who in the name of liberty did just what they pleased.

They continually fluctuated in their numbers. Sailors, deserting ships at other islands, or in boats at sea anywhere in that vicinity, steered for Charles's Isle [Santa Maria/Floreana], as to their sure home of refuge; while, sated with the life of the isle, numbers from time to time crossed the water to the neighboring ones, and there presenting themselves to strange captains as shipwrecked seamen, often succeeded in getting on board vessels bound to the Spanish coast, and having a compassionate purse made up for them on landing there.

One warm night during my first visit to the group, our ship was floating along in languid stillness, when some one on the forecastle shouted "Light ho!" We looked and saw a beacon burning on some obscure land off the beam. Our third mate was not intimate with this part of the world. Going to the captain he said, "Sir, shall I put off in a boat? These must be shipwrecked men."

The captain laughed rather grimly, as, shaking his fist towards the beacon, he rapped out an oath, and said—"No, no, you precious rascals, you don't juggle one of my boats ashore this blessed night. You do well, you thieves—you do benevolently to hoist a light yonder as on a dangerous shoal. It tempts no wise man to pull off and see what's the matter, but bids him steer small and keep off shore—that is Charles's Island [Santa Maria/Floreana]; brace up, Mr. Mate, and keep the light astern."

Eight

Although Melville sets this heartbreaking tale on Norfolk Island [Santa Cruz], the location and landscape he presents are far from that actual spot. They really don't fit any of the islands in the group, as John Woram points out in his delightfully cheeky guide, Charles Darwin Slept Here. *Melville evidently found the island just where he found the story: in his imagination.*

Analysts have noted that the theme of stoic perseverance in the face of overwhelming adversity seen in Billy Budd, *Melville's final work, first presents itself in this story of the widow Hunilla's approach to life on her island.*

This sketch also reflects another theme often seen in Melville's earlier writing, the concepts of "civilized" versus "savage." Here he contrasts the behavior of "civilized" sailors with that of the mixed race indigenous protagonist.

SKETCH EIGHTH.
NORFOLK ISLE AND THE CHOLA WIDOW.

"At last they in an island did espy
A seemly woman sitting by the shore,
That with great sorrow and sad agony
Seemed some great misfortune to deplore;
And loud to them for succor called evermore."
"Black his eye as the midnight sky.
White his neck as the driven snow,
Red his cheek as the morning light;—
Cold he lies in the ground below.
My love is dead,
Gone to his death-bed, ys
All under the cactus tree."
"Each lonely scene shall thee restore,
For thee the tear be duly shed;
Belov'd till life can charm no more,
And mourned till Pity's self be dead."

Far to the northeast of Charles's Isle [Santa Maria/Floreana], sequestered from the rest, lies Norfolk Isle [Santa Cruz]; and, however insignificant to most voyagers, to me, through sympathy, that lone island has become a spot made sacred by the strangest trials of humanity.

It was my first visit to the Encantadas. Two days had been spent ashore in hunting tortoises. There was not time to capture many; so on the third afternoon we loosed our sails. We were just in the act of getting under way, the uprooted anchor yet suspended and invisibly swaying beneath the wave, as the good ship gradually turned her heel to leave the isle behind, when the seaman who heaved with me at the windlass paused suddenly, and directed my attention to something moving on the land, not along the beach, but somewhat back, fluttering from a height.

In view of the sequel of this little story, be it here narrated how it came to pass, that an object which partly from its being so small was quite lost to every other man on board, still caught the eye of my handspike companion.

The rest of the crew, myself included, merely stood up to our spikes in heaving, whereas, unwontedly exhilarated, at every turn of the ponderous windlass, my belted comrade leaped atop of it, with might and main giving a downward, thewey, perpendicular heave, his raised eye bent in cheery animation upon the slowly receding shore.

Being high lifted above all others was the reason he perceived the object, otherwise unperceivable; and this elevation of his eye was owing to the elevation of his spirits; and this again—for truth must out—to a dram of Peruvian pisco, in guerdon for some kindness done, secretly administered to him that morning by our mulatto steward.

Now, certainly, pisco does a deal of mischief in the world; yet seeing that, in the present case, it was the means, though indirect, of rescuing a human being from the most dreadful fate, must we not also needs admit that sometimes pisco does a deal of good?

Glancing across the water in the direction pointed out, I saw some white thing hanging from an inland rock, perhaps half a mile from the sea.

"It is a bird; a white-winged bird; perhaps a—no; it is—it is a handkerchief!"

"Ay, a handkerchief!" echoed my comrade, and with a louder shout apprised the captain.

Quickly now—like the running out and training of a great gun—the long cabin spy-glass was thrust through the mizzen rigging from the high platform of the poop; whereupon a human figure was plainly seen upon the inland rock, eagerly waving towards us what seemed to be the handkerchief.

Our captain was a prompt, good fellow. Dropping the glass, he lustily ran forward, ordering the anchor to be dropped again; hands to stand by a boat, and lower away.

In a half-hour's time the swift boat returned. It went with six and came with seven; and the seventh was a woman.

It is not artistic heartlessness, but I wish I could but draw in crayons; for this woman was a most touching sight; and crayons, tracing softly melancholy lines, would best depict the mournful image of the dark-damasked Chola widow.

Her story was soon told, and though given in her own strange language was as quickly understood; for our captain, from long trading on the Chilian coast, was well versed in the Spanish.

A Cholo, or half-breed Indian woman of Payta in Peru, three years gone by, with her young new-wedded husband Felipe, of pure Castilian blood, and her one only Indian brother, Truxill, Hunilla had taken passage on the main in a French whaler, commanded by a joyous man; which vessel, bound to the cruising grounds beyond the Enchanted Isles, proposed passing close by their vicinity.

The object of the little party was to procure tortoise oil, a fluid which for its great purity and delicacy is held in high estimation wherever known; and it is well known all along this part of the Pacific coast.

With a chest of clothes, tools, cooking utensils, a rude apparatus for trying out the oil, some casks of biscuit, and other things, not omitting two favorite dogs, of which faithful animal all the Cholos are very fond, Hunilla and her companions were safely landed at their chosen place; the Frenchman, according to the contract made ere sailing, engaged to take them off upon returning from a four months' cruise in the westward seas; which interval the three adventurers deemed quite sufficient for their purposes.

On the isle's lone beach they paid him in silver for their passage out, the stranger having declined to carry them at all except upon that condition; though willing to take every means to insure the due fulfillment of his promise. Felipe had striven hard to have this payment put off to the period of the ship's return. But in vain.

Still they thought they had, in another way, ample pledge of the good faith of the Frenchman. It was arranged that the expenses of the passage home should not be payable in silver, but in tortoises; one hundred tortoises ready captured to the returning captain's hand.

These the Cholos meant to secure after their own work was done, against the probable time of the Frenchman's coming back; and no doubt in prospect already felt, that in those hundred tortoises—now somewhere ranging the isle's interior—they possessed one hundred hostages.

Enough: the vessel sailed; the gazing three on shore answered the loud glee of the singing crew; and ere evening, the French craft was hull down in the distant sea, its masts three faintest lines which quickly faded from Hunilla's eye.

The stranger had given a blithesome promise, and anchored it with oaths; but oaths and anchors equally will drag; naught else abides on fickle earth but unkept promises of joy. Contrary winds from out unstable skies, or contrary moods of his more varying mind, or shipwreck and sudden death in solitary waves; whatever was the cause, the blithe stranger never was seen again.

Yet, however dire a calamity was here in store, misgivings of it ere due time never disturbed the Cholos' busy mind, now all intent upon the toilsome matter which had brought them hither. Nay, by swift doom coming like the thief at night, ere seven weeks went by, two of the little party were removed from all anxieties of land or sea. No more they sought to gaze with feverish fear, or still more feverish hope, beyond the present's horizon line; but into the furthest future their own silent spirits sailed.

By persevering labor beneath that burning sun, Felipe and Truxill had brought down to their hut many scores of tortoises, and tried out the oil, when, elated with their good success, and to reward themselves for such hard work, they, too hastily, made a catamaran, or Indian raft, much used on the Spanish main, and merrily started on a fishing trip, just without a long reef with many jagged gaps, running parallel with the shore, about half a mile from it.

By some bad tide or hap, or natural negligence of joyfulness (for though they could not be heard, yet by their gestures they seemed singing at the time) forced in deep water against that iron bar, the ill-made catamaran was overset, and came all to pieces; when dashed by broad-chested swells between their broken logs and the sharp teeth of the reef, both adventurers perished before Hunilla's eyes.

Before Hunilla's eyes they sank. The real woe of this event passed before her sight as some sham tragedy on the stage. She was seated on a rude bower among the withered thickets, crowning a lofty cliff, a little back from the beach. The thickets were so disposed, that in looking upon the sea at large she peered out from among the branches as from the lattice of a high balcony.

But upon the day we speak of here, the better to watch the adventure of those two hearts she loved, Hunilla had withdrawn the branches to one side, and held them so. They formed an oval frame, through which the bluely boundless sea rolled like a painted one. And there, the invisible painter painted to her view the wave-tossed and disjointed raft, its once level logs slantingly upheaved, as raking masts, and the four struggling arms indistinguishable among them; and then all subsided into smooth-flowing creamy waters, slowly drifting the splintered wreck; while first and last, no sound of any sort was heard. Death in a silent picture; a dream of the eye; such vanishing shapes as the mirage shows.

So instant was the scene, so trance-like its mild pictorial effect, so distant from her blasted bower and her common sense of things, that Hunilla gazed and gazed, nor raised a finger or a wail. But as good to sit thus dumb, in stupor staring on that dumb show, for all that otherwise might be done. With half a mile of sea between, how could her two enchanted arms aid those four fated ones? The distance long, the time one sand. After the lightning is beheld, what fool shall stay the thunder-bolt?

Felipe's body was washed ashore, but Truxill's never came; only his gay, braided hat of golden straw—that same sunflower thing he waved to her, pushing from the strand—and now, to the last gallant, it still saluted her. But Felipe's body floated to the marge, with one arm encirclingly outstretched. Lock-jawed in grim death, the lover-husband softly clasped his bride, true to her even in death's dream.

Ah, heaven, when man thus keeps his faith, wilt thou be faithless who created the faithful one? But they cannot break faith who never plighted it.

It needs not to be said what nameless misery now wrapped the lonely widow. In telling her own story she passed this almost entirely over, simply recounting the event. Construe the comment of her features as you might, from her mere words little would you have weened that Hunilla was herself the heroine of her tale. But not thus did she defraud us of our tears. All hearts bled that grief could be so brave.

She but showed us her soul's lid, and the strange ciphers thereon engraved; all within, with pride's timidity, was withheld. Yet was there one exception. Holding out her small olive hand before her captain, she said in mild and slowest Spanish, "Señor, I buried him;" then paused, struggled as against the writhed coilings of a snake, and cringing suddenly, leaped up, repeating in impassioned pain, "I buried him, my life, my soul!"

Doubtless, it was by half-unconscious, automatic motions of her hands, that this heavy-hearted one performed the final office for Felipe, and planted a rude cross of withered sticks—no green ones might be had—at the head of that lonely grave, where rested now in lasting un-complaint and quiet haven he whom untranquil seas had over-thrown.

But some dull sense of another body that should be interred, of another cross that should hallow another grave—unmade as yet—some dull anxiety and pain touching her undiscovered brother, now haunted the oppressed Hunilla. Her hands fresh from the burial earth, she slowly went back to the beach, with unshaped purposes wandering there, her spell-bound eye bent upon the incessant waves. But they bore nothing to her but a dirge, which maddened her to think that murderers should mourn.

As time went by, and these things came less dreamingly to her mind, the strong persuasions of her Romish faith, which sets peculiar store by con-secrated urns, prompted her to resume in waking earnest that pious search which had but been begun as in somnambulism. Day after day, week after week, she trod the cindery beach, till at length a double motive edged every eager glance. With equal longing she now looked for the living and the dead; the brother and the captain; alike vanished, never to return.

Little accurate note of time had Hunilla taken under such emotions as were hers, and little, outside herself, served for calendar or dial. As to poor Crusoe in the self-same sea, no saint's bell pealed forth the lapse of week or month; each day went by unchallenged; no chanticleer announced those sultry dawns, no lowing herds those poison-ous nights. All wonted and steadily recurring sounds, human, or humanized by sweet fellowship with man, but one stirred that torrid trance—the cry of dogs; save which naught but the rolling sea invaded it, an all-pervading monotone; and to the widow that was the least loved voice she could have heard.

No wonder, that as her thoughts now wan-dered to the unreturning ship, and were beaten back again, the hope against hope so struggled in her soul, that at length she desperately said, "Not yet, not yet; my foolish heart runs on too fast." So she forced patience for some further weeks. But to those whom earth's sure indraft draws, patience or impatience is still the same.

Hunilla now sought to settle precisely in her mind, to an hour, how long it was since the ship had sailed; and then, with the same precision, how long a space remained to pass. But this proved im-possible. What present day or month it was she could not say. Time was her labyrinth, in which Hunilla was entirely lost.

And now follows—

Against my own purposes a pause descends upon me here. One knows not whether nature doth not impose some secrecy upon him who has been privy to certain things. At least, it is to be doubted whether it be good to blazon such. If some books are deemed most baneful and their sale forbid, how, then, with deadlier facts, not dreams of doting men? Those whom books will hurt will not be proof against events. Events, not books, should be forbid. But in all things man sows upon the wind, which bloweth just there whither it listeth; for ill or good, man cannot know. Often ill comes from the good, as good from ill.

When Hunilla—

Dire sight it is to see some silken beast long dally with a golden lizard ere she devour. More terrible, to see how feline Fate will sometimes dally with a human soul, and by a nameless magic make it repulse a sane despair with a hope which is but mad. Unwittingly I imp this cat-like thing, sporting with the heart of him who reads; for if he feel not he reads in vain.

—"The ship sails this day, to-day," at last said Hunilla to herself; "this gives me certain time to stand on; without certainty I go mad. In loose ignorance I have hoped and hoped; now in firm knowledge I will but wait. Now I live and no longer perish in bewilderings. Holy Virgin, aid me! Thou wilt waft back the ship. Oh, past length of weary weeks—all to be dragged over—to buy the certainty of to-day, I freely give ye, though I tear ye from me!"

As mariners, tost in tempest on some desolate ledge, patch them a boat out of the remnants of their vessel's wreck, and launch it in the self-same waves, see here Hunilla, this lone shipwrecked soul, out of treachery invoking trust. Humanity, thou strong thing, I worship thee, not in the laureled victor, but in this vanquished one.

Truly Hunilla leaned upon a reed, a real one; no metaphor; a real Eastern reed. A piece of hollow cane, drifted from unknown isles, and found upon the beach, its once jagged ends rubbed smoothly even as by sand-paper; its golden glazing gone.

Long ground between the sea and land, upper and nether stone, the unvarnished substance was filed bare, and wore another polish now, one with itself, the polish of its agony.

Circular lines at intervals cut all round this surface, divided it into six panels of unequal length. In the first were scored the days, each tenth one marked by a longer and deeper notch; the second was scored for the number of sea-fowl eggs for sustenance, picked out from the rocky nests; the third, how many fish had been caught from the shore; the fourth, how many small tortoises found inland; the fifth, how many days of sun; the sixth, of clouds; which last, of the two, was the greater one. Long night of busy numbering, misery's mathematics, to weary her too-wakeful soul to sleep; yet sleep for that was none.

The panel of the days was deeply worn—the long tenth notches half effaced, as alphabets of the blind. Ten thousand times the longing widow had traced her finger over the bamboo—dull flute, which played, on, gave no sound—as if counting birds flown by in air would hasten tortoises creeping through the woods.

After the one hundred and eightieth day no further mark was seen; that last one was the faintest, as the first the deepest.

"There were more days," said our Captain; "many, many more; why did you not go on and notch them, too, Hunilla?"

"Señor, ask me not."

"And meantime, did no other vessel pass the isle?"

"Nay, Señor;—but—"

"You do not speak; but *what*, Hunilla?"

"Ask me not, Señor."

"You saw ships pass, far away; you waved to them; they passed on;—was that it, Hunilla?"

"Señor, be it as you say."

Braced against her woe, Hunilla would not, durst not trust the weakness of her tongue. Then when our Captain asked whether any whale-boats had—

But no, I will not file this thing complete for scoffing souls to quote, and call it firm proof upon their side. The half shall here remain untold. Those two unnamed events which befell Hunilla on this isle, let them abide between her and her God. In nature, as in law, it may be libelous to speak some truths.

Still, how it was that, although our vessel had lain three days anchored nigh the isle, its one human tenant should not have discovered us till just upon the point of sailing, never to revisit so lone and far a spot, this needs explaining ere the sequel come.

The place where the French captain had landed the little party was on the further and opposite end of the isle. There, too, it was that they had afterwards built their hut. Nor did the widow in her solitude desert the spot where her loved ones had dwelt with her, and where the dearest of the twain now slept his last long sleep, and all her plaints awaked him not, and he of husbands the most faithful during life.

Now, high, broken land rises between the opposite extremities of the isle. A ship anchored at one side is invisible from the other. Neither is the isle so small, but a considerable company might wander for days through the wilderness of one side, and never be seen, or their halloos heard, by any stranger holding aloof on the other.

Hence Hunilla, who naturally associated the possible coming of ships with her own part of the isle, might to the end have remained quite ignorant of the presence of our vessel, were it not for a mysterious presentiment, borne to her, so our mariners averred, by this isle's enchanted air. Nor did the widow's answer undo the thought.

"How did you come to cross the isle this morning, then, Hunilla?" said our Captain.

"Señor, something came flitting by me. It touched my cheek, my heart, Señor."

"What do you say, Hunilla?"

"I have said, Señor, something came through the air."

It was a narrow chance. For when in crossing the isle Hunilla gained the high land in the centre, she must then for the first have perceived our masts, and also marked that their sails were being loosed, perhaps even heard the echoing chorus of the windlass song. The strange ship was about to sail, and she behind.

With all haste she now descends the height on the hither side, but soon loses sight of the ship among the sunken jungles at the mountain's base. She struggles on through the withered branches, which seek at every step to bar her path, till she comes to the isolated rock, still some way from the water. This she climbs, to reassure herself. The ship is still in plainest sight.

But now, worn out with over tension, Hunilla all but faints; she fears to step down from her giddy perch; she is fain to pause, there where she is, and as a last resort catches the turban from her head, unfurls and waves it over the jungles towards us.

During the telling of her story the mariners formed a voiceless circle round Hunilla and the Captain; and when at length the word was given to man the fastest boat, and pull round to the isle's thither side, to bring away Hunilla's chest and the tortoise-oil, such alacrity of both cheery and sad obedience seldom before was seen.

Little ado was made. Already the anchor had been recommitted to the bottom, and the ship swung calmly to it.

But Hunilla insisted upon accompanying the boat as indispensable pilot to her hidden hut. So being refreshed with the best the steward could supply, she started with us. Nor did ever any wife of the most famous admiral, in her husband's barge, receive more silent reverence of respect than poor Hunilla from this boat's crew.

Rounding many a vitreous cape and bluff, in two hours' time we shot inside the fatal reef; wound into a secret cove, looked up along a green many-gabled lava wall, and saw the island's solitary dwelling.

It hung upon an impending cliff, sheltered on two sides by tangled thickets, and half-screened from view in front by juttings of the rude stairway, which climbed the precipice from the sea. Built of canes, it was thatched with long, mildewed grass. It seemed an abandoned hay-rick, whose haymakers were now no more. The roof inclined but one way; the eaves coming to within two feet of the ground.

And here was a simple apparatus to collect the dews, or rather doubly-distilled and finest winnowed rains, which, in mercy or in mockery, the night-skies sometimes drop upon these blighted Encantadas. All along beneath the eaves, a spotted sheet, quite weather-stained, was spread, pinned to short, upright stakes, set in the shallow sand. A small clinker, thrown into the cloth, weighed its middle down, thereby straining all moisture into a calabash placed below.

This vessel supplied each drop of water ever drunk upon the isle by the Cholos. Hunilla told us the calabash, would sometimes, but not often, be half filled overnight. It held six quarts, perhaps. "But," said she, "we were used to thirst. At sandy Payta, where I live, no shower from heaven ever fell; all the water there is brought on mules from the inland vales."

Tied among the thickets were some twenty moaning tortoises, supplying Hunilla's lonely larder; while hundreds of vast tableted black bucklers, like displaced, shattered tomb-stones of dark slate, were also scattered round. These were the skeleton backs of those great tortoises from which Felipe and Truxill had made their precious oil. Several large calabashes and two goodly kegs were filled with it. In a pot near by were the caked crusts of a quantity which had been permitted to evaporate. "They meant to have strained it off next day," said Hunilla, as she turned aside.

I forgot to mention the most singular sight of all, though the first that greeted us after landing.

Some ten small, soft-haired, ringleted dogs, of a beautiful breed, peculiar to Peru, set up a concert of glad welcomings when we gained the beach, which was responded to by Hunilla. Some of these dogs had, since her widowhood, been born upon the isle, the progeny of the two brought from Payta.

Owing to the jagged steeps and pitfalls, tortuous thickets, sunken clefts and perilous intricacies of all sorts in the interior, Hunilla, admonished by the loss of one favorite among them, never allowed these delicate creatures to follow her in her occasional birds'-nests climbs and other wanderings; so that, through long habituation, they offered not to follow, when that morning she crossed the land, and her own soul was then too full of other things to heed their lingering behind.

Yet, all along she had so clung to them, that, besides what moisture they lapped up at early daybreak from the small scoop-holes among the adjacent rocks, she had shared the dew of her calabash among them; never laying by any considerable store against those prolonged and utter droughts which, in some disastrous seasons, warp these isles.

Having pointed out, at our desire, what few things she would like transported to the ship—her chest, the oil, not omitting the live tortoises which she intended for a grateful present to our Captain—we immediately set to work, carrying them to the boat down the long, sloping stair of deeply-shadowed rock.

While my comrades were thus employed, I looked and Hunilla had disappeared.

It was not curiosity alone, but, it seems to me, something different mingled with it, which prompted me to drop my tortoise, and once more gaze slowly around.

I remembered the husband buried by Hunilla's hands. A narrow pathway led into a dense part of the thickets. Following it through many mazes, I came out upon a small, round, open space, deeply chambered there.

The mound rose in the middle; a bare heap of finest sand, like that unverdured heap found at the bottom of an hour-glass run out. At its head stood the cross of withered sticks; the dry, peeled bark still fraying from it; its transverse limb tied up with rope, and forlornly adroop in the silent air.

Hunilla was partly prostrate upon the grave; her dark head bowed, and lost in her long, loosened Indian hair; her hands extended to the cross-foot, with a little brass crucifix clasped between; a crucifix worn featureless, like an ancient graven knocker long plied in vain. She did not see me, and I made no noise, but slid aside, and left the spot.

A few moments ere all was ready for our going, she reappeared among us. I looked into her eyes, but saw no tear. There was something which seemed strangely haughty in her air, and yet it was the air of woe. A Spanish and an Indian grief, which would not visibly lament. Pride's height in vain abased to proneness on the rack; nature's pride subduing nature's torture.

Like pages the small and silken dogs surrounded her, as she slowly descended towards the
beach. She caught the two most eager creatures in
her arms:—"Mia Teeta! Mia Tomoteeta!" and fon-
dling them, inquired how many could we take on
board.

The mate commanded the boat's crew; not a
hard-hearted man, but his way of life had been such
that in most things, even in the smallest, simple
utility was his leading motive.

"We cannot take them all, Hunilla; our sup-
plies are short; the winds are unreliable; we may be
a good many days going to Tombez. So take those
you have, Hunilla; but no more."

She was in the boat; the oarsmen, too, were
seated; all save one, who stood ready to push off
and then spring himself. With the sagacity of their
race, the dogs now seemed aware that they were in
the very instant of being deserted upon a barren
strand.

The gunwales of the boat were high; its
prow—presented inland—was lifted; so owing to the
water, which they seemed instinctively to shun, the
dogs could not well leap into the little craft. But
their busy paws hard scraped the prow, as it had
been some farmer's door shutting them out from
shelter in a winter storm. A clamorous agony of
alarm. They did not howl, or whine; they all but
spoke.

"Push off! Give way!" cried the mate. The
boat gave one heavy drag and lurch, and next moment shot swiftly from the beach, turned on her
heel, and sped. The dogs ran howling along the water's marge; now pausing to gaze at the flying boat,
then motioning as if to leap in chase, but mysteri-

ously withheld themselves; and again ran howling along the beach.

Had they been human beings, hardly would they have more vividly inspired the sense of desolation. The oars were plied as confederate feathers of two wings. No one spoke. I looked back upon the beach, and then upon Hunilla, but her face was set in a stern dusky calm. The dogs crouching in her lap vainly licked her rigid hands.

She never looked behind her: but sat motionless, till we turned a promontory of the coast and lost all sights and sounds astern. She seemed as one who, having experienced the sharpest of mortal pangs, was henceforth content to have all lesser heartstrings riven, one by one.

To Hunilla, pain seemed so necessary, that pain in other beings, though by love and sympathy made her own, was unrepiningly to be borne. A heart of yearning in a frame of steel. A heart of

108

earthly yearning, frozen by the frost which falleth from the sky.

The sequel is soon told. After a long passage, vexed by calms and baffling winds, we made the little port of Tombez in Peru, there to recruit the ship. Payta was not very distant. Our captain sold the tortoise oil to a Tombez merchant; and adding to the silver a contribution from all hands, gave it to our silent passenger, who knew not what the mariners had done.

The last seen of lone Hunilla she was passing into Payta town, riding upon a small gray ass; and before her on the ass's shoulders, she eyed the jointed workings of the beast's armorial cross.

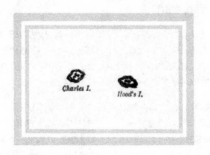

Nine

Again Melville draws on island lore, combined with his own fictional elements (such as the intense malevolence of the main character), to tell the story of Irishman Patrick "Mad Pat" Watkins, the archipelago's first settler.

He sets the tale on Hood's Island [Espanola] but acknowledges that Captain David Porter (of USS Essex fame), who also told the story, placed it on Charles's Island [Santa Maria/Floreana] as do modern historians.

Analysts suggest that Melville uses his own version of this story to equate the desire to keep slaves with absolute evil, as he held strong anti-slavery views in this pre-Civil War era.

The "Sycorax" Oberlus mentions comes from Shakespeare's play The Tempest, *also set on a nearly deserted island. In the play, Sycorax, a powerful witch, was the mother of Caliban, the island's only (semi-) human inhabitant.*

SKETCH NINTH.
HOOD'S ISLE AND THE HERMIT OBERLUS.

"That darkesome glen they enter, where they find
That cursed man low sitting on the ground,
Musing full sadly in his sullein mind;
His griesly lockes long gronen and unbound,
Disordered hong about his shoulders round,
And hid his face, through which his hollow eyne
Lookt deadly dull, and stared as astound;
His raw-bone cheekes, through penurie and pine,
Were shronke into the jawes, as he did never dine.
His garments nought but many ragged clouts,
With thornes together pind and patched reads,
The which his naked sides he wrapt abouts."

Southeast of Crossman's Isle [several possible islets] lies Hood's Isle [Espanola], or McCain's Beclouded Isle; and upon its south side is a vitreous cove with a wide strand of dark pounded black lava, called Black Beach, or Oberlus's Landing. It might fitly have been styled Charon's.

It received its name from a wild white creature who spent many years here; in the person of a European bringing into this savage region qualities more diabolical than are to be found among any of the surrounding cannibals.

About half a century ago, Oberlus deserted at the above-named island, then, as now, a solitude. He built himself a den of lava and clinkers, about a mile from the Landing, subsequently called after him, in a vale, or expanded gulch, containing here and there among the rocks about two acres of soil capable of rude cultivation; the only place on the isle not too blasted for that purpose. Here he succeeded in raising a sort of degenerate potatoes and pumpkins, which from time to time he exchanged with needy whalemen passing, for spirits or dollars.

His appearance, from all accounts, was that of the victim of some malignant sorceress; he seemed to have drunk of Circe's cup; beast-like; rags insufficient to hide his nakedness; his befreckled skin blistered by continual exposure to the sun; nose flat; countenance contorted, heavy, earthy; hair and beard unshorn, profuse, and of fiery red.

He struck strangers much as if he were a volcanic creature thrown up by the same convulsion which exploded into sight the isle. All bepatched and coiled asleep in his lonely lava den among the mountains, he looked, they say, as a heaped drift of withered leaves, torn from autumn trees, and so left in some hidden nook by the whirling halt for an instant of a fierce night-wind, which then ruthlessly sweeps on, somewhere else to repeat the capricious act.

It is also reported to have been the strangest sight, this same Oberlus, of a sultry, cloudy morning, hidden under his shocking old black tarpaulin hat, hoeing potatoes among the lava. So warped and crooked was his strange nature, that the very handle of his hoe seemed gradually to have shrunk and twisted in his grasp, being a wretched bent stick, elbowed more like a savage's war-sickle than a civilized hoe-handle.

It was his mysterious custom upon a first encounter with a stranger ever to present his back; possibly, because that was his better side, since it revealed the least. If the encounter chanced in his garden, as it sometimes did—the new-landed strangers going from the sea-side straight through

the gorge, to hunt up the queer green-grocer reported doing business here—Oberlus for a time
hoed on, unmindful of all greeting, jovial or bland;
as the curious stranger would turn to face him, the
recluse, hoe in hand, as diligently would avert himself; bowed over, and sullenly revolving round his
murphy hill. Thus far for hoeing.

When planting, his whole aspect and all his
gestures were so malevolently and uselessly sinister
and secret, that he seemed rather in act of dropping
poison into wells than potatoes into soil. But among
his lesser and more harmless marvels was an idea
he ever had, that his visitors came equally as well
led by longings to behold the mighty hermit Oberlus in his royal state of solitude, as simply, to obtain
potatoes, or find whatever company might be upon
a barren isle.

It seems incredible that such a being should
possess such vanity; a misanthrope be conceited;
but he really had his notion; and upon the strength
of it, often gave himself amusing airs to captains.
But after all, this is somewhat of a piece with the
well-known eccentricity of some convicts, proud of
that very hatefulness which makes them notorious.

At other times, another unaccountable
whim would seize him, and he would long dodge
advancing strangers round the clinkered corners of
his hut; sometimes like a stealthy bear, he would
slink through the withered thickets up the mountains, and refuse to see the human face.

Except his occasional visitors from the sea, for a long period, the only companions of Oberlus were the crawling tortoises; and he seemed more than degraded to their level, having no desires for a time beyond theirs, unless it were for the stupor brought on by drunkenness.

But sufficiently debased as he appeared, there yet lurked in him, only awaiting occasion for discovery, a still further proneness. Indeed, the sole superiority of Oberlus over the tortoises was his possession of a larger capacity of degradation; and along with that, something like an intelligent will to it.

Moreover, what is about to be revealed, perhaps will show, that selfish ambition, or the love of rule for its own sake, far from being the peculiar infirmity of noble minds, is shared by beings which have no mind at all. No creatures are so selfishly tyrannical as some brutes; as any one who has observed the tenants of the pasture must occasionally have observed.

"This island's mine by Sycorax my mother," said Oberlus to himself, glaring round upon his haggard solitude. By some means, barter or theft—for in those days ships at intervals still kept touching at his Landing—he obtained an old musket, with a few charges of powder and ball.

Possessed of arms, he was stimulated to enterprise, as a tiger that first feels the coming of its claws. The long habit of sole dominion over every object round him, his almost unbroken solitude, his never encountering humanity except on terms of misanthropic independence, or mercantile craftiness, and even such encounters being comparatively but rare; all this must have gradually nourished in him a vast idea of his own importance, together with a pure animal sort of scorn for all the rest of the universe.

The unfortunate Creole, who enjoyed his brief term of royalty at Charles's Isle [Santa Maria/Floreana] was perhaps in some degree influenced by not unworthy motives; such as prompt other adventurous spirits to lead colonists into distant regions and assume political preeminence over them. His summary execution of many of his Peruvians is quite pardonable, considering the desperate characters he had to deal with; while his offering canine battle to the banded rebels seems under the circumstances altogether just.

But for this King Oberlus and what shortly follows, no shade of palliation can be given. He acted out of mere delight in tyranny and cruelty, by virtue of a quality in him inherited from Sycorax his mother. Armed now with that shocking blunderbuss, strong in the thought of being master of that horrid isle, he panted for a chance to prove his potency upon the first specimen of humanity which should fall unbefriended into his hands.

Nor was he long without it. One day he spied a boat upon the beach, with one man, a negro, standing by it. Some distance off was a ship, and Oberlus immediately knew how matters stood. The vessel had put in for wood, and the boat's crew had gone into the thickets for it. From a convenient spot he kept watch of the boat, till presently a straggling company appeared loaded with billets. Throwing these on the beach, they again went into the thickets, while the negro proceeded to load the boat.

Oberlus now makes all haste and accosts the negro, who, aghast at seeing any living being inhabiting such a solitude, and especially so horrific a one, immediately falls into a panic, not at all lessened by the ursine suavity of Oberlus, who begs the favor of assisting him in his labors.

The negro stands with several billets on his shoulder, in act of shouldering others; and Oberlus, with a short cord concealed in his bosom, kindly proceeds to lift those other billets to their place. In so doing, he persists in keeping behind the negro, who, rightly suspicious of this, in vain dodges about to gain the front of Oberlus; but Oberlus dodges also; till at last, weary of this bootless attempt at treachery, or fearful of being surprised by the remainder of the party, Oberlus runs off a little space to a bush, and fetching his blunderbuss, savagely commands the negro to desist work and follow him. He refuses. Whereupon, presenting his piece, Oberlus snaps at him.

Luckily the blunderbuss misses fire; but by this time, frightened out of his wits, the negro, upon a second intrepid summons, drops his billets, surrenders at discretion, and follows on. By a narrow defile familiar to him, Oberlus speedily removes out of sight of the water.

On their way up the mountains, he exultingly informs the negro, that henceforth he is to work for him, and be his slave, and that his treatment would entirely depend on his future conduct.

But Oberlus, deceived by the first impulsive cowardice of the black, in an evil moment slackens his vigilance. Passing through a narrow way, and perceiving his leader quite off his guard, the negro, a powerful fellow, suddenly grasps him in his arms, throws him down, wrests his musketoon from him, ties his hands with the monster's own cord, shoulders him, and returns with him down to the boat.

When the rest of the party arrive, Oberlus is carried on board the ship. This proved an Englishman, and a smuggler; a sort of craft not apt to be over-charitable. Oberlus is severely whipped, then handcuffed, taken ashore, and compelled to make known his habitation and produce his property. His potatoes, pumpkins, and tortoises, with a pile of dollars he had hoarded from his mercantile operations were secured on the spot.

But while the too vindictive smugglers were busy destroying his hut and garden, Oberlus makes his escape into the mountains, and conceals himself there in impenetrable recesses, only known to himself, till the ship sails, when he ventures back, and by means of an old file which he sticks into a tree, contrives to free himself from his handcuffs.

Brooding among the ruins of his hut, and the desolate clinkers and extinct volcanoes of this outcast isle, the insulted misanthrope now meditates a signal revenge upon humanity, but conceals his purposes. Vessels still touch the Landing at times; and by-and-by Oberlus is enabled to supply them with some vegetables.

Warned by his former failure in kidnapping strangers, he now pursues a quite different plan. When seamen come ashore, he makes up to them like a free-and-easy comrade, invites them to his hut, and with whatever affability his red-haired grimness may assume, entreats them to drink his liquor and be merry.

But his guests need little pressing; and so, soon as rendered insensible, are tied hand and foot, and pitched among the clinkers, are there concealed till the ship departs, when, finding themselves entirely dependent upon Oberlus, alarmed at his changed demeanor, his savage threats, and above all, that shocking blunderbuss, they willingly enlist under him, becoming his humble slaves, and Oberlus the most incredible of tyrants. So much so, that two or three perish beneath his initiating process.

He sets the remainder—four of them—to breaking the caked soil; transporting upon their backs loads of loamy earth, scooped up in moist clefts among the mountains; keeps them on the roughest fare; presents his piece at the slightest hint of insurrection; and in all respects converts them into reptiles at his feet—plebeian garter-snakes to this Lord Anaconda.

At last, Oberlus contrives to stock his arsenal with four rusty cutlasses, and an added supply of powder and ball intended for his blunderbuss. Remitting in good part the labor of his slaves, he now approves himself a man, or rather devil, of great abilities in the way of cajoling or coercing others into acquiescence with his own ulterior designs, however at first abhorrent to them.

But indeed, prepared for almost any eventual evil by their previous lawless life, as a sort of ranging Cow-Boys of the sea, which had dissolved within them the whole moral man, so that they were ready to concrete in the first offered mould of baseness now; rotted down from manhood by their hopeless misery on the isle; wonted to cringe in all things to their lord, himself the worst of slaves; these wretches were now become wholly corrupted to his hands. He used them as creatures of an inferior race; in short, he gaffles his four animals, and makes murderers of them; out of cowards fitly manufacturing bravos.

Now, sword or dagger, human arms are but artificial claws and fangs, tied on like false spurs to the fighting cock. So, we repeat, Oberlus, czar of the isle, gaffles his four subjects; that is, with intent of glory, puts four rusty cutlasses into their hands. Like any other autocrat, he had a noble army now.

It might be thought a servile war would hereupon ensue. Arms in the hands of trodden slaves? how indiscreet of Emperor Oberlus! Nay, they had but cutlasses—sad old scythes enough—he a blunderbuss, which by its blind scatterings of all sorts of boulders, clinkers, and other scoria would annihilate all four mutineers, like four pigeons at one shot.

Besides, at first he did not sleep in his accustomed hut; every lurid sunset, for a time, he might have been seen wending his way among the riven mountains, there to secrete himself till dawn in some sulphurous pitfall, undiscoverable to his gang; but finding this at last too troublesome, he now each evening tied his slaves hand and foot, hid the cutlasses, and thrusting them into his barracks, shut to the door, and lying down before it, beneath a rude shed lately added, slept out the night, blunderbuss in hand.

It is supposed that not content with daily parading over a cindery solitude at the head of his fine army, Oberlus now meditated the most active mischief; his probable object being to surprise some passing ship touching at his dominions, massacre the crew, and run away with her to parts unknown. While these plans were simmering in his head, two ships touch in company at the isle, on the opposite side to his; when his designs undergo a sudden change.

The ships are in want of vegetables, which Oberlus promises in great abundance, provided they send their boats round to his landing, so that the crews may bring the vegetables from his garden; informing the two captains, at the same time, that his rascals—slaves and soldiers—had become so abominably lazy and good-for-nothing of late, that he could not make them work by ordinary inducements, and did not have the heart to be severe with them.

The arrangement was agreed to, and the boats were sent and hauled upon the beach. The crews went to the lava hut; but to their surprise nobody was there. After waiting till their patience was exhausted, they returned to the shore, when lo, some stranger—not the Good Samaritan either—seems to have very recently passed that way. Three of the boats were broken in a thousand pieces, and the fourth was missing. By hard toil over the mountains and through the clinkers, some of the strangers succeeded in returning to that side of the isle where the ships lay, when fresh boats are sent to the relief of the rest of the hapless party.

However amazed at the treachery of Oberlus, the two captains, afraid of new and still more mysterious atrocities—and indeed, half imputing such strange events to the enchantments associated with these isles—perceive no security but in instant flight; leaving Oberlus and his army in quiet possession of the stolen boat.

On the eve of sailing they put a letter in a keg, giving the Pacific Ocean intelligence of the affair, and moored the keg in the bay. Some time subsequent, the keg was opened by another captain chancing to anchor there, but not until after he had dispatched a boat round to Oberlus's Landing. As may be readily surmised, he felt no little inquietude till the boat's return: when another letter was handed him, giving Oberlus's version of the affair. This precious document had been found pinned half-mildewed to the clinker wall of the sulphurous and deserted hut. It ran as follows: showing that Oberlus was at least an accomplished writer, and no mere boor; and what is more, was capable of the most tristful eloquence.

"Sir: I am the most unfortunate ill-treated gentleman that lives. I am a patriot, exiled from my country by the cruel hand of tyranny.

"Banished to these Enchanted Isles, I have again and again besought captains of ships to sell me a boat, but always have been refused, though I offered the handsomest prices in Mexican dollars. At length an opportunity presented of possessing myself of one, and I did not let it slip.

"I have been long endeavoring, by hard labor and much solitary suffering, to accumulate something to make myself comfortable in a virtuous though unhappy old age; but at various times have been robbed and beaten by men professing to be Christians.

124

"To-day I sail from the Enchanted group in the good boat Charity bound to the Feejee Isles.

"FATHERLESS OBERLUS.

"*P.S.*—Behind the clinkers, nigh the oven, you will find the old fowl. Do not kill it; be patient; I leave it setting; if it shall have any chicks, I hereby bequeath them to you, whoever you may be. But don't count your chicks before they are hatched."

The fowl proved a starveling rooster, reduced to a sitting posture by sheer debility.

Oberlus declares that he was bound to the Feejee Isles; but this was only to throw pursuers on a false scent. For, after a long time, he arrived, alone in his open boat, at Guayaquil. As his miscreants were never again beheld on Hood's Isle [Espanola], it is supposed, either that they perished for want of water on the passage to Guayaquil, or, what is quite as probable, were thrown overboard by Oberlus, when he found the water growing scarce.

From Guayaquil Oberlus proceeded to Payta; and there, with that nameless witchery peculiar to some of the ugliest animals, wound himself into the affections of a tawny damsel; prevailing upon her to accompany him back to his Enchanted Isle; which doubtless he painted as a Paradise of flowers, not a Tartarus of clinkers.

But unfortunately for the colonization of Hood's Isle [Espanola] with a choice variety of animated nature, the extraordinary and devilish aspect of Oberlus made him to be regarded in Payta as a highly suspicious character. So that being found concealed one night, with matches in his pocket, under the hull of a small vessel just ready to be launched, he was seized and thrown into jail.

The jails in most South American towns are generally of the least wholesome sort. Built of huge cakes of sun-burnt brick, and containing but one room, without windows or yard, and but one door heavily grated with wooden bars, they present both within and without the grimmest aspect. As public edifices they conspicuously stand upon the hot and dusty Plaza, offering to view, through the gratings, their villainous and hopeless inmates, burrowing in all sorts of tragic squalor. And here, for a long time, Oberlus was seen; the central figure of a mongrel and assassin band; a creature whom it is religion to detest, since it is philanthropy to hate a misanthrope.

Note.—They who may be disposed to question the possibility of the character above depicted, are referred to the 2d vol. of Porter's *Voyage into the Pacific*, where they will recognize many sentences, for expedition's sake derived verbatim from thence, and incorporated here; the main difference—save a few passing reflections—between the two accounts being, that the present writer has added to Porter's facts accessory ones picked up in the Pacific from reliable sources; and where facts conflict, has naturally preferred his own authorities to Porter's.

As, for instance, *his* authorities place Oberlus on Hood's Isle [Espanola]: Porter's, on Charles's Isle [Santa Maria/Floreana]. The letter found in the hut is also somewhat different; for while at the Encantadas he was informed that, not only did it evince a certain clerkliness, but was full of the strangest satiric effrontery which does not adequately appear in Porter's version. I accordingly altered it to suit the general character of its author.

Ten

Perhaps Melville was sympathetic to sailors in this sketch who deserted their ships because he had done the same himself. In July 1842, after more than a year on the whaler Acushnet, the twenty-three year old future author grew disgusted with its harsh conditions and jumped ship in the Marquesas Islands, evidently with few repercussions.

After living among the reputedly cannibalistic natives for a month, Melville joined the crew of one, then another, whaler eventually landing in Honolulu where he worked as a clerk for four months.

In August 1843 he signed on to the warship USS United States as a Navy seaman. It reached Boston—the end of his enlistment—in October 1844.

After entertaining friends and relatives with his exotic stories for several months, Melville turned to writing as a career, making use of his South Seas adventures to engage the reading public.

In this sketch Melville accurately describes the struggle for water that men ashore in the Galapagos Islands encountered. Fresh water was, and remains, scarce on most of the islands. Chatham Island [San Christobal] where the Acushnet anchored November 19 through 25, 1841 to restock before heading to whaling grounds off the South American coast, was the only reliable source of enough fresh water to supply a ship.

The grave Melville describes on James's Island [San Salvador/Santiago] belonged to the promising young Midshipman John S. Cowan of the USS Essex, the ship featured in the fifth sketch, who was killed in a duel with a fellow officer on August 10, 1812.

SKETCH TENTH.
RUNAWAYS, CASTAWAYS, SOLITARIES, GRAVE-STONES, ETC.

"And all about old stocks and stubs of trees,
Whereon nor fruit nor leaf was ever seen,
Did hang upon ragged knotty knees,
On which had many wretches hanged been."

Some relics of the hut of Oberlus partially remain to this day at the head of the clinkered valley. Nor does the stranger, wandering among other of the Enchanted Isles, fail to stumble upon still other solitary abodes, long abandoned to the tortoise and the lizard.

Probably few parts of earth have, in modern times, sheltered so many solitaries. The reason is, that these isles are situated in a distant sea, and the vessels which occasionally visit them are mostly all whalers, or ships bound on dreary and protracted voyages, exempting them in a good degree from both the oversight and the memory of human law.

Such is the character of some commanders and some seamen, that under these untoward circumstances, it is quite impossible but that scenes of unpleasantness and discord should occur between them. A sullen hatred of the tyrannic ship will seize the sailor, and he gladly exchanges it for isles, which, though blighted as by a continual sirocco and burning breeze, still offer him, in their labyrinthine interior, a retreat beyond the possibility of capture.

131

To flee the ship in any Peruvian or Chilian port, even the smallest and most rustical, is not unattended with great risk of apprehension, not to speak of jaguars. A reward of five pesos sends fifty dastardly Spaniards into the wood, who, with long knives, scour them day and night in eager hopes of securing their prey.

Neither is it, in general, much easier to escape pursuit at the isles of Polynesia. Those of them which have felt a civilizing influence present the same difficulty to the runaway with the Peruvian ports, the advanced natives being quite as mercenary and keen of knife and scent as the retrograde Spaniards; while, owing to the bad odor in which all Europeans lie, in the minds of aboriginal savages who have chanced to hear aught of them, to desert the ship among primitive Polynesians, is, in most cases, a hope not unforlorn.

Hence the Enchanted Isles become the voluntary tarrying places of all sorts of refugees; some of whom too sadly experience the fact, that flight from tyranny does not of itself insure a safe asylum, far less a happy home.

Moreover, it has not seldom happened that hermits have been made upon the isles by the accidents incident to tortoise-hunting. The interior of most of them is tangled and difficult of passage beyond description; the air is sultry and stifling; an intolerable thirst is provoked, for which no running stream offers its kind relief. In a few hours, under an equatorial sun, reduced by these causes to entire exhaustion, woe betide the straggler at the Enchanted Isles! Their extent is such-as to forbid an adequate search, unless weeks are devoted to it.

The impatient ship waits a day or two; when, the missing man remaining undiscovered, up goes a stake on the beach, with a letter of regret, and a keg of crackers and another of water tied to it, and away sails the craft.

Nor have there been wanting instances where the inhumanity of some captains has led them to wreak a secure revenge upon seamen who have given their caprice or pride some singular offense. Thrust ashore upon the scorching marl, such mariners are abandoned to perish outright, unless by solitary labors they succeed in discovering some precious dribblets of moisture oozing from a rock or stagnant in a mountain pool.

I was well acquainted with a man, who, lost upon the Isle of Narborough [Fernandina], was brought to such extremes by thirst, that at last he only saved his life by taking that of another being. A large hair-seal came upon the beach. He rushed upon it, stabbed it in the neck, and then throwing himself upon the panting body quaffed at the living wound; the palpitations of the creature's dying heart injected life into the drinker.

Another seaman, thrust ashore in a boat upon an isle at which no ship ever touched, owing to its peculiar sterility and the shoals about it, and from which all other parts of the group were hidden—this man, feeling that it was sure death to remain there, and that nothing worse than death menaced him in quitting it, killed seals, and inflating their skins, made a float, upon which he transported himself to Charles's Island [Santa Maria/Floreana], and joined the republic there.

But men, not endowed with courage equal to such desperate attempts, find their only resource in forthwith seeking some watering-place, however precarious or scanty; building a hut; catching tortoises and birds; and in all respects preparing for a hermit life, till tide or time, or a passing ship arrives to float them off.

At the foot of precipices on many of the isles, small rude basins in the rocks are found, partly filled with rotted rubbish or vegetable decay, or overgrown with thickets, and sometimes a little moist; which, upon examination, reveal plain tokens of artificial instruments employed in hollowing them out, by some poor castaway or still more miserable runaway. These basins are made in places where it was supposed some scanty drops of dew might exude into them from the upper crevices.

The relics of hermitages and stone basins are not the only signs of vanishing humanity to be found upon the isles. And, curious to say, that spot which of all others in settled communities is most animated, at the Enchanted Isles presents the most dreary of aspects.

And though it may seem very strange to talk of post-offices in this barren region, yet post-offices are occasionally to be found there. They consist of a stake and a bottle. The letters being not only sealed, but corked. They are generally deposited by captains of Nantucketers for the benefit of passing fishermen, and contain statements as to what luck they had in whaling or tortoise-hunting. Frequently, however, long months and months, whole years glide by and no applicant appears. The stake rots and falls, presenting no very exhilarating object.

If now it be added that grave-stones, or rather grave-boards, are also discovered upon some of the isles, the picture will be complete.

Upon the beach of James's Isle [San Salvador/Santiago], for many years, was to be seen a rude finger-post, pointing inland. And, perhaps, taking it for some signal of possible hospitality in this otherwise desolate spot—some good hermit living there with his maple dish—the stranger would follow on in the path thus indicated, till at last he would come out in a noiseless nook, and find his only welcome, a dead man—his sole greeting the inscription over a grave. Here, in 1813, fell, in a daybreak duel, a lieutenant of the U.S. frigate *Essex*, aged twenty-one: attaining his majority in death.

It is but fit that, like those old monastic institutions of Europe, whose inmates go not out of their own walls to be inurned, but are entombed there where they die, the Encantadas, too, should bury their own dead, even as the great general monastery of earth does hers.

It is known that burial in the ocean is a pure necessity of sea-faring life, and that it is only done when land is far astern, and not clearly visible from the bow. Hence, to vessels cruising in the vicinity of the Enchanted Isles, they afford a convenient Potter's Field. The interment over, some good-natured forecastle poet and artist seizes his paint-brush, and inscribes a doggerel epitaph. When, after a long lapse of time, other good-natured seamen chance to come upon the spot, they usually make a table of the mound, and quaff a friendly can to the poor soul's repose.

As a specimen of these epitaphs, take the following, found in a bleak gorge of Chatham Isle [San Cristobal]:—

"Oh, Brother Jack, as you pass by,
As you are now, so once was I.
Just so game, and just so gay,
But now, alack, they've stopped my pay.
No more I peep out of my blinkers,
Here I be—tucked in with clinkers!"

~ ~ ~

Melville began his first sketch of the Galapagos Islands with an image of cinders. He ends this last sketch with one of clinkers. Yet in spite of his dark approach to his subject, the wonder, mystery, and uniqueness of these Enchanted Isles still manage to emerge from his writing, even after 150 years.

Afterword

Melville did regain readers with The Encantadas. *The public greeted his magazine articles with enthusiasm. Other short pieces sold well to* Putnam's *and occasionally to* Harper's New Monthly Magazine. *Once again Melville began to make money, and more consistently than he ever had with his novels. Unfortunately, his success did not continue for long.*

In 1856 he put the ten Enchanted Isles sketches together with other short pieces including "Bartleby the Scrivener" and "Benito Cereno" publishing them as The Piazza Tales. *Critics reviewed the book favorably, especially* The Encantadas *portion, but books were harder to sell than magazines. It did poorly.*

Then Putnam's, *his main source of income, went out of business.*

Financial setbacks, marital difficulties, family tragedies, depression, and alcohol abuse plagued Melville throughout the rest of his life. The decline in popularity of his writing continued.

In 1866 Melville was able to obtain the post of New York City customs inspector which he held for the next nineteen years. Although he continued writing, mostly poetry in later years, he was nearly forgotten by the time of his death in 1891.

It was not until the 1920s that a revival of interest in his work lead to worldwide acclaim, especially for Moby-Dick *and his last work,* Billy Budd, Sailor.

About the Illustrations

The period drawings included in this work are images, or details of images, from an illustrated 1890 edition of Charles Darwin's *The Voyage of the Beagle*, a narrative first published in 1839, about the time Herman Melville was sailing the South Pacific.

Moses Michelsohn took all the photographs for this book in the Galapagos Islands.

A Note on Island Names

Each of the Galapagos Islands has several names, a heritage of their centuries of human history.

Names assigned by English buccaneers in the 1600s generally superseded those used by early Spanish explorers, except for the name of the archipelago itself, "The Galapagos Islands" (referring to the saddle shape of the tortoises' shells). Fray Tomas de Berlanga, Bishop of Panama, first referred the islands in this fashion in 1535. (Actually the official name is Archipelago de Colon but no one uses this.)

Captain William Ambrosia Cowley, an English buccaneer, explorer, adventurer, and writer who visited the Galápagos Islands while sailing around the world in the mid-1600s, named individual islands after British royalty and aristocrats. As he published the first widely used chart of the archipelago in 1684, these names quickly came into common usage.

When Ecuador annexed the archipelago in 1832 the new government assigned each island an official Spanish name, often that of a Catholic saint. These are the names commonly used today, although a few islands picked up other common names along the way.

The primary islands described in *The Encantadas* are:

Melville's Name	Today's Name(s)
Albemarle	Isabela
Barrington	Santa Fe
Charles's	Santa Maria, Floreana
Hood's	Espanola
James's	San Salvador, Santiago
Narborough	Fernandina
Norfolk	Santa Cruz

Melville also mentions Abington (Pinta), Brattle (Tortuga), Chatham (San Cristobal), Cowley's Enchanted (Cowley), Crossman's (several possible islets), Duncan (Pinzon), Jervis (Rabida) and Wood's (also Santa Maria).

Acknowledgements

"The Geography of Herman Melville" in John Woram's enjoyable book *Charles Darwin Slept Here* provided a variety of interesting information as did *Critical Companion to Herman Melville* by Carl Rollyson, Lisa Paddock, and April Gentry. Hershel Parker's two volume *Herman Melville: A Biography* furnished detailed information about Melville's time in the Galapagos Islands, as well as the months he spent writing "The Encantadas." All quotes from contemporary reviews of Melville's novels came from the highly detailed and immensely readable *Melville, A Biography* by Laurie Robertson-Lorant.

We thank Dr. David Hastings for leading a great trip to the Galapagos Islands, Aaron Michelsohn for his valuable editorial assistance, and Larry Michelsohn for his continued support of this and all our projects.

About the Authors

Over the course of his 72 years (1819-1891) **Herman Melville** wrote novels, short stories, essays, and poetry in the genre that has been called "dark romanticism." His *Moby-Dick*, published in 1851, is considered by many to be the best novel ever written. It, like *The Encantadas* and his well respected novella *Billy Budd*, draws on his shipboard experiences in the South Seas as a young man. Born in New York City, Melville did much of his writing in the western Massachusetts town of Pittsfield, but later moved back to New York. His grave, in Woodland Cemetery in the Bronx, attracts thousands of visitors each year.

Lynn Michelsohn has felt an affinity for Herman Melville since spending time in Great Barrington, a town neighboring his Pittsfield home. An "indoor researcher," she enjoys tracking down details of interesting places and characters. She and her husband, who calls himself a "recovering attorney," spend their time in Santa Fe and West Palm Beach.

Photographer **Moses Michelsohn,** like Melville, found tortoises on the Galapagos Islands fascinating, but they couldn't divert him from his primary research interest: frogs. After studying tropical anurans in Ecuador and Costa Rica, he began investigating tree frog populations in the southeastern United States. His hobbies include wildlife photography, drawing, and cultivating native plants around his Tallahassee home.